ISBN 978-1-334-16431-6
PIBN 10566260

MARK, THE MATCH BOY;

OR,

RICHARD HUNTER'S WARD.

BY

HORATIO ALGER, JR.,

AUTHOR OF "RAGGED DICK," "FAME AND FORTUNE," "FRANK'S CAMPAIGN," "PAUL PRESCOTT'S CHARGE," "CHARLIE CODMAN'S CRUISE," ETC.

THE JOHN C. WINSTON CO.,

PHILADELPHIA,

CHICAGO, TORONTO.

To

JAMES ALGER

THIS VOLUME IS INSCRIBED,

BY HIS

AFFECTIONATE BROTHER.

PREFACE.

"MARK, THE MATCH BOY," is the third volume of the "Ragged Dick Series," and, like its predecessors, aims to describe a special phase of street life in New York. While it is complete in itself, several characters are introduced who have figured conspicuously in the preceding volumes; and the curiosity as to their future history, which has been expressed by many young readers, will be found to be gratified in the present volume.

The author has observed with pleasure the increased public attention which has been drawn to the condition of these little waifs of city life, by articles in our leading magazines, and in other ways; and hopes that the result will be to strengthen and assist the philanthropic efforts which are making to rescue them from their vagabond condition, and train them up to be useful members of society. That his own efforts have been received with so large a measure of public favor, not limited to the young readers for whom the series is especially written, the author desires to express his grateful thanks.

NEW YORK, April, 1869.

MARK, THE MATCH BOY;

OR,

RICHARD HUNTER'S WARD.

CHAPTER I.

RICHARD HUNTER AT HOME.

"FOSDICK," said Richard Hunter, "what was the name of that man who owed your father two thousand dollars, which he never paid him?"

"Hiram Bates," answered Fosdick, in some surprise. "What made you think of him?"

"I thought I remembered the name. He moved out West, didn't he?"

"So I heard at the time."

"Do you happen to remember where? Out West is a very large place."

"I do not know exactly, but I think it was Milwaukie."

"Indeed!" exclaimed Richard Hunter, in visible

excitement. "Well, Fosdick, why don't you try to get the debt paid?"

"Of what use would it be? How do I know he is living in Milkaukie now? If I should write hin a letter, there isn't much chance of my ever getting an answer."

"Call and see him."

"What, go out to Milwaukie on such a wild-goose chase as that? I can't think what you are driving at, Dick."

"Then I'll tell you, Fosdick. Hiram Bates is now in New York."

"How do you know?" asked Fosdick, with an expression of mingled amazement and incredulity.

"I'll show you."

Richard Hunter pointed to the list of hotel arrivals in the "Evening Express," which he held in his hand. Among the arrivals at the Astor House occurred the name of Hiram Bates, from Mil waukie.

"If I am not mistaken," he said, "that is the name of your father's debtor."

"I don't know but you are right," said Fosdick, thoughtfully.

"He must be prosperous if he stops at a high-priced hotel like the Astor."

"Yes, I suppose so. How much good that money would have done my poor father," he added, with a sigh.

"How much good it will do you, Fosdick."

Fosdick shook his head. "I would sell out my chance of getting it for ten dollars," he said.

"I would buy it at that price if I wanted to make money out of you; but I don't. I advise you to attend to this matter at once."

"What can I do?" asked Fosdick, who seemed at a loss to understand his companion's meaning.

"There is only one thing to do," said Dick, promptly. "Call on Mr. Bates this evening at the hotel. Tell him who you are, and hint that you should like the money."

"I haven't got your confidence, Dick. I shouldn't know how to go about it. Do you really think it would do any good? He might think I was impertinent."

"Impertinent to ask payment of a just debt! I don't see it in that light. I think I shall have to go with you."

"I wish you would, — that is, if you really think there is any use in going."

"You mustn't be so bashful if you want to get on in the world, Fosdick. As long as there's a chance of getting even a part of it, I advise you to make the attempt."

"Well, Dick, I'll be guided by your advice."

"Two thousand dollars would be a pretty good windfall for you."

"That's true enough, considering that I only get eight dollars a week."

"I wish you got more."

"So do I, for one particular reason."

"What is that?"

"I don't feel satisfied to have you pay ten dollars a week towards our board, while I pay only six."

"Didn't you promise not to say anything more about that?" said Dick, reproachfully.

"But I can't help *thinking* about it. If we had stayed at our old boarding-house in Bleecker Street, I could have paid my full share."

"But this is a nicer room."

"Much nicer. If I only paid my half, I should be glad of the chance."

"Well, I'll promise you one thing If Mr. ! ates pays you the two thousand dollars, you may pay your half of the expense."

"Not much chance of that, Dick."

"We can tell better after calling at the Astor House. Get on your coat and we'll start."

While the boys, — for the elder of the two is but eighteen — are making preparations to go out, a few explanations may be required by the reader. Those who have read "Ragged Dick" and "Fame and Fortune," — the preceding volumes of this series, — will understand that less than three years before Richard Hunter was an ignorant and ragged bootblack about the streets, and Fosdick, though possessing a better education, was in the same business. By a series of upward steps, partly due to good fortune, but largely to his own determination to improve, and hopeful energy, Dick had now become a book-keeper in the establishment of Rockwell & Cooper, on Pearl Street, and possessed the confidence and good wishes of the firm in a high degree.

Fosdick was two years younger, and, though an excellent boy, was less confident, and not so well fitted as his friend to contend with the difficulties of life, and fight his way upward. He was employed in Henderson's hat and cap store on Broadway, and was at present earning a salary of eight dollars a week. As the two paid sixteen dollars weekly for their board, Fosdick would have had nothing left if he had paid his full share. But Richard Hunter at first insisted on paying eleven dollars out of the sixteen, leaving his friend but five to pay. To this Fosdick would not agree, and was with difficulty prevailed upon at last to allow Richard to pay ten; but he had always felt a delicacy about this, although he well knew how gladly his friend did it.

The room which they now occupied was situated in St. Mark's Place, which forms the eastern portion of Eighth Street. It was a front room on the third floor, and was handsomely furnished. There was a thick carpet, of tasteful figure, on the floor. Between the two front windows was a handsome bureau, surmounted by a large mirror. There was a comfortable sofa, chairs covered with hair-cloth, a centre-table covered with books, crimson curtains, which gave a warm and cosey look to the room when lighted up in the evening, and all the accessories of a well-furnished room which is used at the same time as parlor and chamber. This, with an excellent table, afforded a very agreeable home to the boys, — a home which, in these days, would cost considerably more, but for which, at the time of which I write, sixteen dollars was a fair price.

It may be thought that, considering how recently Richard Hunter had been a ragged bootblack, content to sleep in boxes and sheltered doorways, and live at the cheapest restaurants, he had become very luxurious in his tastes. Why did he not get a cheaper boarding-place, and save up the difference in price? No doubt this consideration will readily suggest itself to the minds of some of my young readers.

As Richard Hunter had a philosophy of his own on this subject, I may as well explain it here. He had observed that those young men who out of economy contented themselves with small and cheerless rooms, in which there was no provision for a fire, were driven in the evening to the streets, theatres, and hotels, for the comfort which they could not find at home. Here they felt obliged to spend money to an extent of which they probably were not themselves fully aware, and in the end wasted consideraly more than the two or three dollars a week extra which would have provided them with a comfortable home. But this was not all. In the roamings spent outside many laid the foundation of wrong habits, which eventually led to ruin or shortened their lives. They lost all the chances of improvement which they might have secured by study at home in the long winter evenings, and which in the end might have qualified them for posts of higher responsibility, and with a larger compensation.

Richard Hunter was ambitious. He wanted to rise to an honorable place in the community, and he meant to earn it by hard study. So Fosdick and he were in the habit of spending a portion of every evening in improving reading or study. Occasionally he went to some place of amusement, but he enjoyed thoroughly the many evenings when, before a cheerful fire, with books in their hands, his room-mate and himself were adding to their stock of knowledge. The boys had for over a year taken lessons in French and mathematics, and were now able to read the French language with considerable ease.

"What's the use of moping every evening in your

room?" asked a young clerk who occupied a hall bedroom adjoining.

"I don't call it moping. I enjoy it," was the reply.

"You don't go to a place of amusement once a month."

"I go as often as I like."

"Well, you're a queer chap. You pay such a thundering price for board. You could go to the theatre four times a week without its costing you any more, if you would take a room like mine."

"I know it; but I'd rather have a nice, comfortable room to come home to."

"Are you studying for a college professor?" asked the other, with a sneer.

"I don't know," said Dick, good-humoredly; "but I'm open to proposals, as the oyster remarked. If you know any first-class institution that would like a dignified professor, of extensive acquirements, just mention me, will you?"

So Richard Hunter kept on his way, indifferent to the criticisms which his conduct excited in the minds of young men of his own age. He looked farther than they, and knew that if he wanted to succeed in life, and win the respect of his fellow-men, he must do something else than attend theatres, and spend his evenings in billiard saloons. Fosdick, who was a quiet, studious boy, fully agreed with his friend in his views of life, and by his companionship did much to strengthen and confirm Richard in his resolution. He was less ambitious than Dick, and perhaps loved study more for its own sake.

With these explanations we shall now be able to start fairly in our story.

CHAPTER II.

AT THE ASTOR HOUSE.

THE two friends started from their room about seven o'clock, and walked up to Third Avenue, where they jumped on board a horse-car, and within half an hour were landed at the foot of the City Hall Park, opposite Beekman Street. From this point it was necessary only to cross the street to the Astor House.

The Astor House is a massive pile of gray stone, and has a solid look, as if it might stand for hundreds of years. When it was first erected, a little more than thirty years since, it was considered far up town, but now it is far down town, so rapid has been the growth of the city.

Richard Hunter ascended the stone steps with a firm step, but Henry Fosdick lingered behind.

"Do you think we had better go up, Dick?" he said irresolutely.

"Why not?"

"I feel awkward about it."

"There is no reason why you should. The money belongs to you rightfully, as the repre sentative of your father, and it is worth trying for."

"I suppose you are right, but I shan't know what to say."

"I'll help you alcng if I find you need it. Come along."

Those who possess energy and a strong will generally gain their point, and it was so with Richard Hunter. They entered the hotel, and, ascending some stone steps, found themselves on the main floor, where the reading-room, clerk's office, and dining-room are located.

Dick, to adopt the familiar name by which his companion addressed him, stepped up to the desk, and drew towards him the book of arrivals. After a brief search he found the name of "Hiram Bates, Milwaukie, Wis.," towards the top of the left-hand page.

"Is Mr. Bates in?" he inquired of the clerk, pointing to the name.

"I will send and inquire, if you will write your name on this card."

Dick thought it would be best to send his own name, as that of Fosdick might lead Mr. Bates to guess the business on which they had come.

He accordingly wrote the name,

Richard Hunter,

in his handsomest handwriting, and handed it to the clerk.

That functionary touched a bell. The summons was answered by a servant.

"James, go to No. 147, and see if Mr. Bates is in. If he is, give him this card."

The messenger departed at once, and returned quickly.

"The gentleman is in, and would be glad to have Mr. Hunter walk up."

"Come along, Fosdick," said Dick, in a low voice.

Fosdick obeyed, feeling very nervous. Following the servant upstairs, they soon stood before No. 147.

James knocked.

"Come in," was heard from the inside, and the two friends entered.

They found themselves in a comfortably furnished room. A man of fifty-five, rather stout in build, and with iron-gray hair, rose from his chair before the fire, and looked rather inquiringly. He seemed rather surprised to find that there were two visitors, as well as at the evident youth of both.

"Mr. Hunter?" he said, inquiringly, looking from one to the other.

"That is my name," said Dick, promptly.

"Have I met you before? If so, my memory is at fault."

"No, sir, we have never met."

"I presume you have business with me. Be seated, if you please."

"First," said Dick, "let me introduce my friend Henry Fosdick."

"Fosdick!" repeated Hiram Bates, with a slight tinge of color.

"I think you knew my father," said Fosdick, nervously.

"Your father was a printer, — was he not?" inquired Mr. Bates.

"Yes, sir."

"I do remember him. Do you come from him?"

Fosdick shook his head.

"He has been dead for two years," he said. sadly.

"Dead!" repeated Hiram Bates, as if shocked. "Indeed, I am sorry to hear it."

He spoke with evident regret, and Henry Fosdick, whose feelings towards his father's debtor had not been very friendly, noticed this, and was softened by it.

"Did he die in poverty, may I ask?" inquired Mr. Bates, after a pause.

"He was poor," said Fosdick; "that is, he had nothing laid up; but his wages were enough to support him and myself comfortably."

"Did he have any other family?"

"No, sir; my mother died six years since, and I had no brothers or sisters."

"He left no property then?"

"No, sir."

"Then I suppose he was able to make no provision for you?"

"No, sir."

"But you probably had some relatives who came forward and provided for you?"

"No, sir; I had no relatives in New York."

"What then did you do? Excuse my questions, but I have a motive in asking."

"My father died suddenly, having fallen from a Brooklyn ferry-boat and drowned. He left nothing, and I knew of nothing better to do than to go into the streets as a boot-black."

"Surely you are not in that business now?" said Mr. Bates, glancing at Fosdick's neat dress.

"No, sir; I was fortunate enough to find a friend,"—here Fosdick glanced at Dick,—"who helped me along, and encouraged me to apply for a place in a Broadway store. I have been there now for a year and a half."

"What wages do you get? Excuse my curiosity, but your story interests me."

"Eight dollars a week."

"And do you find you can live comfortably on that?"

"Yes, sir; that is, with the assistance of my friend here."

"I am glad you have a friend who is able and willing to help you."

"It is not worth mentioning," said Dick, modestly "I have received as much help from him as he has from me."

"I see at any rate that you are good friends, and a good friend is worth having. May I ask, Mr. Fosdick, whether you ever heard your father refer to me in any way?"

"Yes, sir."

"You are aware, then, that there were some money arrangements between us?"

"I have heard him say that you had two thousand dollars of his, but that you failed, and that it was lost."

"He informed you rightly. I will tell you the particulars, if you are not already aware of them."

"I should be very glad to hear them, sir. My father died so suddenly that I never knew anything more than that you owed him two thousand dollars."

"Five years since," commenced Mr. Bates, "I was a broker in Wall Street. As from my business

I was expected to know the best investments. Some persons brought me money to keep for them, and I either agreed to pay them a certain rate of interest, or gave them an interest in my speculations. Among the persons was your father. The way in which I got acquainted with him was this: Having occasion to get some prospectuses of a new company printed, I went to the office with which he was connected. There was some error in the printing, and he was sent to my office to speak with me about it. When our business was concluded, he waited a moment, and then said, 'Mr. Bates, I have saved up two thousand dollars in the last ten years, but I don't know much about investments, and I should consider it a favor if you would advise me.'

"'I will do so with pleasure,' I said. 'If you desire it I will take charge of it for you, and either allow you six per cent. interest, or give you a share of the profits I may make from investing it.'

"Your father said that he should be glad to have me take the money for him, but he would prefer regular interest to uncertain profits. The next day he brought the money, and put it in my hands. To confess the truth I was glad to have him do so, for I was engaged in extensive speculations, and thought I could make use of it to advantage. For a year I paid him the interest regularly. Then there came a great catastrophe, and I found my brilliant speculations were but bubbles, which broke and left me but a mere pittance, instead of the hundred thousand dollars which I considered myself worth. Of course those who had placed money in my hands suffered, and among them your father. I confess that I regretted his loss as much as that of any one, for I liked his straightforward manner, and was touched by his evident confidence in me."

Mr. Bates paused a moment and then resumed:—

"I left New York, and went to Milwaukie. Here I was obliged to begin life anew, or nearly so, for I only carried a thousand dollars out with me. But I have been greatly prospered since then. I took warning by my past failures, and have succeeded, by care and good fortune, in accumulating nearly as large a fortune as the one of which I once thought myself possessed. When fortune began to smile upon me I thought of your father, and tried through an agent to find him out. But he reported to me that his name was not to be found either in the New York or Brooklyn Directory, and I was too busily engaged to come on myself, and make inquiries. But I am glad to find that his son is living, and that I yet have it in my power to make restitution."

Fosdick could hardly believe his ears. Was he after all to receive the money which he had supposed irrevocably lost?

As for Dick it is not too much to say that he felt even more pleased at the prospective good fortune of his friend than if it had fallen to himself.

CHAPTER III.

FOSDICK'S FORTUNE.

MR. BATES took from his pocket a memorandum book, and jotted down a few figures in it.

"As nearly as I can remember," he said, "it is four years since I ceased paying interest on the money which your father entrusted to me. The rate I agreed to pay was six per cent. How much will that amount to?"

"Principal and interest two thousand four hundred and eighty dollars," said Dick, promptly.

Fosdick's breath was almost taken away as he heard this sum mentioned. Could it be possible that Mr. Bates intended to pay him as much as this? Why, it would be a fortune.

"Your figures would be quite correct, Mr. Hunter," said Mr. Bates, "but for one consideration. You forget that your friend is entitled to compound interest, as no interest has been paid for four years Now, as you are no doubt used to figures, I will leave you to make the necessary correction."

Mr. Bates tore a leaf from his memorandum book as he spoke, and handed it with a pencil to Richard Hunter.

Dick made a rapid calculation, and reported two thousand five hundred and twenty-four dollars.

"It seems, then, Mr. Fosdick," said Mr. Bates, "that I am your debtor to a very considerable amount."

"You are very kind, sir," said Fosdick; "but I shall be quite satisfied with the two thousand dollars without any interest."

"Thank you for offering to relinquish the interest; but it is only right that I should pay it. I have had the use of the money, and I certainly would not wish to defraud you of a penny of the sum which it took your father ten years of industry to accumulate. I wish he were living now to see justice done his son."

"So do I," said Fosdick, earnestly. "I beg your pardon, sir," he said, after a moment's pause.

"Why?" asked Mr. Bates in a tone of surprise.

"Because," said Fosdick, "I have done you injustice I thought you failed in order to make money, and intended to cheat my father out of his savings. That made me feel hard towards you."

"You were justified in feeling so," said Mr. Bates. "Such cases are so common that I am not surprised at your opinion of me. I ought to have explained my position to your father, and promised to make restitution whenever it should be in my power. But at the time I was discouraged, and could not foresee the favorable turn which my affairs have since taken. Now," he added, with a change of voice, "we will arrange about the payment of this money."

"Do not pay it until it is convenient, Mr. Bates," said Fosdick.

"Your proposal is kind, but scarcely business-like, Mr. Fosdick," said Mr. Bates. "Fortunately it will occasion me no inconvenience to pay you at once I have not the ready money with me as you may suppose, but I will give you a cheque for the amount upon the Broadway Bank, with which I have an account; and it will be duly honored on presentation to-morrow. You may in return make out a receipt in full for the debt and interest. Wait a moment. I will ring for writing materials."

These were soon brought by a servant of the hotel

and Mr. Bates filled in a cheque for the sum specified above, while Fosdick, scarcely knowing whether he was awake or dreaming, made out a receipt to which he attached his name.

"Now," said Mr. Bates, "we will exchange documents."

Fosdick took the cheque, and deposited it carefully in his pocket-book.

"It is possible that payment might be refused to a boy like you, especially as the amount is so large. At what time will you be disengaged to-morrow?"

"I am absent from the store from twelve to one for dinner."

"Very well, come to the hotel as soon as you are free, and I will accompany you to the bank, and get the money for you. I advise you, however, to leave it there on deposit until you have a chance to invest it."

"How would you advise me to invest it, sir?" asked Fosdick.

"Perhaps you cannot do better than buy shares of some good bank. You will then have no care except to collect your dividends twice a year."

"That is what I should like to do," said Fosdick. 'What bank would you advise?"

"The Broadway, Park, or Bank of Commerce, are all good banks. I will attend to the matter for you, if you desire it."

"I should be very glad if you would, sir."

"Then that matter is settled," said Mr. Bates. "I wish I could as easily settle another matter which has brought me to New York at this time, and which, I confess, occasions me considerable perplexity."

The boys remained respectfully silent, though not without curiosity as to what this matter might be.

Mr. Bates seemed plunged in thought for a short time. Then speaking, as if to himself, he said, in a low voice, "Why should I not tell them? Perhaps they may help me."

"I believe," he said, "I will take you into my confidence. You may be able to render me some assistance in my perplexing business."

"I shall be very glad to help you if I can," said Dick.

"And I also," said Fosdick.

"I have come to New York in search of my grandson," said Mr. Bates.

"Did he run away from home?" asked Dick.

"No, he has never lived with me. Indeed, I may add that I have never seen him since he was an infant."

The boys looked surprised.

"How old is he now?" asked Fosdick.

'He must be about ten years old. But I see that I must give you the whole story of what is a painful passage in my life, or you will be in no position to help me.

"You must know, then, that twelve years since I considered myself rich, and lived in a handsome house up town. My wife was dead, but I had an only daughter, who I believe was generally considered attractive, if not beautiful. I had set my heart upon her making an advantageous marriage; that is, marrying a man of wealth and social position. I had in my employ a clerk, of excellent business abilities, and of good personal appearance, whom I sometimes invited to my house when I entertained company. His name was John Talbot. I never suspected that there was any danger of my daughter's falling in love with the young man, until one day he came to me and overwhelmed me with surprise by asking her hand in marriage.

"You can imagine that I was very angry, whether justly or not I will not pretend to say. I dismissed the young man from my employ, and informed him that never, under any circumstances, would I consent to his marrying Irene. He was a high-spirited young man, and, though he did not answer me, I saw by the expression of his face that he meant to persevere in his suit.

"A week later my daughter was missing. She left behind a letter stating that she could not give up John Talbot, and by the time I read the letter she would be his wife. Two days later a Philadelphia paper was sent me containing a printed notice of their marriage, and the same mail brought me a joint letter from both, asking my forgiveness.

"I had no objections to John Talbot except his poverty; but my ambitious hopes were disappointed, and I felt the blow severely. I returned the letter to the address given, accompanied by a brief line to Irene, to the effect that I disowned her, and would never more acknowledge her as my daughter.

"I saw her only once after that. Two years after she appeared suddenly in my library, having been admitted by the servant, with a child in her arms. But I hardened my heart against her, and though she besought my forgiveness, I refused it, and requested her to leave the house. I cannot forgive myself when I think of my unfeeling severity. But it is too late too redeem the past. As far as I can I would like to atone for it.

"A month since I heard that both Irene and her husband were dead, the latter five years since, but that the child, a boy, is still living, probably in deep poverty. He is my only descendant, and I seek to find him, hoping that he may be a joy and solace to me in the old age which will soon be upon me. It is for the purpose of tracing him that I have come to New York. When you, turning to Fosdick, referred to your being compelled to resort to the streets, and the hard life of a boot-black, the thought came to me that my grandson may be reduced to a similar extremity. It would be hard indeed that he should grow up ignorant, neglected, and subject to every privation, when a comfortable and even luxurious home awaits him, if he can only be found."

"What is his name?" inquired Dick.

"My impression is, that he was named after his father, John Talbot. Indeed, I am quite sure that my daughter wrote me to this effect in a letter which I returned after reading."

"Have you reason to think he is in New York?"

"My information is, that his mother died here a year since. It is not likely that he has been able to leave the city."

"He is about ten years old?"

"I used to know most of the boot-blacks and news-boys when I was in the business," said Dick, reflectively; "but I cannot recall that name."

"Were you ever in the business, Mr. Hunter?" asked Mr. Bates, in surprise.

"Yes," said Richard Hunter, smiling; "I used to be one of the most ragged boot-blacks in the city. Don't you remember my Washington coat, and Napoleon pants, Fosdick?"

"I remember them well."

"Surely that was many years ago?"

"It is not yet two years since I gave up blacking boots."

"You surprise me Mr. Hunter," said Mr. Bates

"I congratulate you on your advance in life. Such a rise shows remarkable energy on your part."

"I was lucky," said Dick, modestly. "I found some good friends who helped me along. But about your grandson: I have quite a number of friends among the street-boys, and I can inquire of them whether any boy named John Talbot has joined their ranks since my time."

"I shall be greatly obliged to you if you will," said Mr. Bates. "But it is quite possible that circumstances may have led to a change of name, so that it will not do to trust too much to this. Even if no boy bearing that name is found, I shall feel that there is this possibility in my favor."

"That is true," said Dick. "It is very common for boys to change their name. Some can't remember whether they ever had any names, and pick one out to suit themselves, or perhaps get one from those they go with. There was one boy I knew named 'Horace Greeley.' Then there were 'Fat Jack,' 'Pickle Nose,' 'Cranky Jim,' 'Tickle-me-foot,' and plenty of others* You knew some of them, didn't you, Fosdick?"

* See sketches of the Formation of the Newsboys' Lodging-house by C. L. Brace, Secretary of the Children's Aid Society.

"I knew 'Fat Jack' and 'Tickle-me-Foot,'" answered Fosdick.

"This of course increases the difficulty of finding and identifying the boy," said Mr. Bates. "Here," he said, taking a card photograph from his pocket, "is a picture of my daughter at the time of her marriage. I have had these taken from a portrait in my possession."

"Can you spare me one?" asked Dick. "It may help me to find the boy."

"I will give one to each of you. I need not say that I shall feel most grateful for any service you may be able to render me, and will gladly reimburse any expenses you may incur, besides paying you liberally for your time. It will be better perhaps for me to leave fifty dollars with each of you to defray any expenses you may be at."

"Thank you," said Dick; "but I am well supplied with money, and will advance whatever is needful, and if I succeed I will hand in my bill."

Fosdick expressed himself in a similar way, and after some further conversation he and Dick rose to go.

"I congratulate you on your wealth, Fosdick,'

said Dick, when they were outside. "You're richer than I am now."

"I never should have got this money but for you, Dick. I wish you'd take some of it."

"Well, I will. You may pay my fare home on the horse-cars."

"But really I wish you would."

But this Dick positively refused to do, as might have been expected. He was himself the owner of two up-town lots, which he eventually sold for five thousand dollars, though they only cost him one, and had three hundred dollars besides in the bank. He agreed, however, to let Fosdick henceforth bear his share of the expenses of board, and this added two dollars a week to the sum he was able to lay up.

CHAPTER IV.

A DIFFICULT COMMISSION.

IT need hardly be said that Fosdick was punctual to his appointment at the Astor House on the following day.

He found Mr. Bates in the reading-room, looking over a Milwaukie paper.

"Good-morning, Mr. Fosdick," he said, extending his hand. "I suppose your time is limited, therefore it will be best for us to go at once to the bank."

"You are very kind, sir, to take so much trouble on my account," said Fosdick.

"We ought all to help each other," said Mr. Bates. "I believe in that doctrine, though I have not always lived up to it. On second thoughts," he added, as they got out in front of the hotel, "if you approve of my suggestions about the purchase of bank shares, it may not be necessary to go to the bank, as you can take this cheque in payment."

"Just as you think best, sir. I can depend upon your judgment, as you know much more of such things than I."

"Then we will go at once to the office of Mr. Ferguson, a Wall Street broker, and an old friend of mine. There we will give an order for some bank shares."

Together the two walked down Broadway until they reached Trinity Church, which fronts the entrance to Wall Street. Here then they crossed the street, and soon reached the office of Mr. Ferguson.

Mr. Ferguson, a pleasant-looking man with sandy hair and whiskers, came forward and shook Mr. Bates cordially by the hand.

"Glad to see you, Mr. Bates," he said. "Where have you been for the last four years?"

"In Milwaukie. I see you are at the old place."

"Yes, plodding along as usual. How do you like the West?"

"I have found it a good place for business, though

I am not sure whether I like it as well to live in as New York."

"Shan't you come back to New York some time?"

Mr. Bates shook his head.

"My business ties me to Milwaukie," he said. "I doubt if I ever return."

"Who is this young man?" said the broker, looking at Fosdick. "He is not a son of yours I think?"

"No; I am not fortunate enough to have a son. He is a young friend who wants a little business done in your line and, I have accordingly brought him to you."

"We will do our best for him. What is it?"

"He wants to purchase twenty shares in some good city bank. I used to know all about such matters when I lived in the city, but I am out of the way of such knowledge now."

"Twenty shares, you said?"

"Yes."

"It happens quite oddly that a party brought in only fifteen minutes since twenty shares in the —— Bank to dispose of. It is a good bank, and I don't know that he can do any better than take them."

"Yes, it is a good bank. What interest does it pay now?"

"Eight per cent."*

"That is good. What is the market value of the stock?"

"It is selling this morning at one hundred and twenty."

"Twenty shares then will amount to twenty-four hundred dollars."

"Precisely."

"Well, perhaps we had better take them. What do you say, Mr. Fosdick?"

"If you advise it, sir, I shall be very glad to do so."

"Then the business can be accomplished at once, as the party left us his signature, authorizing the transfer."

The transfer was rapidly effected. The broker's commission of twenty-five cents per share amounted to five dollars. It was found on paying this, added to the purchase money, that one hundred and nine-

* This was before the war. Now most of the National Banks in New York pay ten per cent., and some even higher.

teen dollars remained, — the cheque being for two thousand five hundred and twenty-four dollars.

The broker took the cheque, and returned this sum, which Mr. Bates handed to Fosdick.

"You may need this for a reserve fund," he said "to draw upon if needful until your dividend comes due. The bank shares will pay you probably one hundred and sixty dollars per year."

"One hundred and sixty dollars!" repeated Fosdick, in surprise. "That is a little more than three dollars a week."

"Yes."

"It will be very acceptable, as my salary at the store is not enough to pay my expenses."

"I would advise you not to break in upon your capital if you can avoid it," said Mr. Bates. "By and by, if your salary increases, you may be able to add the interest yearly to the principal, so that it may be accumulating till you are a man, when you may find it of use in setting you up in business."

"Yes, sir; I will remember that. But I can hardly realize that I am really the owner of twenty bank shares."

"No doubt it seems sudden to you. Don t let it make you extravagant. Most boys of your age would need a guardian, but you have had so much experience in taking care of yourself, that I think you can get along without one."

"I have my friend Dick to advise me," said Fosdick.

"Mr. Hunter seems quite a remarkable young man," said Mr. Bates. "I can hardly believe that his past history has been as he gave it."

"It is strictly true, sir. Three years ago he could not read or write."

"If he continues to display the same energy, I can predict for him a prominent position in the future."

"I am glad to hear you say so, sir. Dick is a very dear friend of mine."

"Now, Mr. Fosdick, it is time you were thinking of dinner. I believe this is your dinner hour?"

"Yes, sir."

"And it is nearly over. You must be my guest to-day. I know of a quiet little lunch room near by, which I used to frequent some years ago when I was in business on this street. We will drop in there and I think you will be able to get through in time."

Fosdick could not well decline the invitation, but accompanied Mr. Bates to the place referred to, where he had a better meal than he was accustomed to. It was finished in time, for as the clock on the city hall struck one, he reached the door of Henderson's store.

Fosdick could not very well banish from his mind the thoughts of his extraordinary change of fortune, and I am obliged to confess that he did not discharge his duties quite as faithfully as usual that afternoon. I will mention one rather amusing instance of his preoccupation of mind.

A lady entered the store, leading by the hand her son Edwin, a little boy of seven.

"Have you any hats that will fit my little boy?" she said.

"Yes, ma'am," said Fosdick, absently, and brought forward a large-sized man's hat, of the kind popularly known as "stove-pipe."

"How will this do?" asked Fosdick.

"I don't want to wear such an ugly hat as that," said Edwin, in dismay.

The lady looked at Fosdick as if she had very strong doubts of his sanity. He saw his mistake, and, coloring deeply, said, in a hurried tone, "Excuse me; I was thinking of something else."

The next selection proved more satisfactory, and Edwin went out of the store feeling quite proud of his new hat.

Towards the close of the afternoon, Fosdick was surprised at the entrance of Mr. Bates. He came up to the counter where he was standing, and said, "I am glad I have found you in. I was not quite sure if this was the place where you were employed."

"I am glad to see you, sir," said Fosdick.

"I have just received a telegram from Milwaukie," said Mr. Bates, "summoning me home immediately on matters connected with business. I shall not therefore be able to remain here to follow up the search upon which I had entered. As you and your friend have kindly offered your assistance, I am going to leave the matter in your hands, and will authorize you to incur any expenses you may deem advisable, and I will gladly reimburse you whether you succeed or not."

Fosdick assured him that they would spare no efforts, and Mr. Bates, after briefly thanking him, and giving him his address, hurried away, as he had determined to start on his return home that very night.

CHAPTER V.

INTRODUCES MARK, THE MATCH BOY.

It was growing dark, though yet scarcely six o'clock, for the day was one of the shortest in the year, when a small boy, thinly clad, turned down Frankfort Street on the corner opposite French's Hotel. He had come up Nassau Street, passing the "Tribune" Office and the old Tammany Hall, now superseded by the substantial new "Sun" building.

He had a box of matches under his arm, of which very few seemed to have been sold. He had a weary, spiritless air, and walked as if quite tired. He had been on his feet all day, and was faint with hunger, having eaten nothing but an apple to sustain his strength. The thought that he was near his journey's end did not seem to cheer him much. Why this should be so will speedily appear.

He crossed William Street, passed Gold Street, and turned down Vandewater Street, leading out of

Frankfort's Street on the left. It is in the form of a short curve, connecting with that most crooked of all New York avenues, Pearl Street. He paused in front of a shabby house, and went upstairs. The door of a room on the third floor was standing ajar. He pushed it open, and entered, not without a kind of shrinking.

A coarse-looking woman was seated before a scanty fire. She had just thrust a bottle into her pocket after taking a copious draught therefrom, and her flushed face showed that this had long been a habit with her.

"Well, Mark, what luck to-night?" she said, in a husky voice.

"I didn't sell much," said the boy.

"Didn't sell much? Come here," said the woman, sharply.

Mark came up to her side, and she snatched the box from him, angrily.

"Only three boxes gone?" she repeated. "What have you been doing all day?"

She added to the question a coarse epithet which I shall not repeat.

"I tried to sell them, indeed I did, Mother Watson,

indeed I did," said the boy, earnestly, "but every-body had bought them already."

"You didn't try," said the woman addressed as Mother Watson. "You're too lazy, that's what's the matter. You don't earn your salt. Now give me the money."

Mark drew from his pocket a few pennies, and handed to her.

She counted them over, and then, looking up sharply, said, with a frown, "There's a penny short. Where is it?"

"I was so hungry," pleaded Mark, "that I bought an apple, — only a little one."

"You bought an apple, did you?" said the woman, menacingly. "So that's the way you spend my money, you little thief?"

"I was so faint and hungry," again pleaded the boy.

"What business had you to be hungry? Didn't you have some breakfast this morning?"

"I had a piece of bread."

"That's more than you earned. You'll eat me out of house and home, you little thief! But I'll pay you off. I'll give you something to take away your appetite. You won't be hungry any more, I reckon."

She dove her flabby hand into her pocket, and produced a strap, at which the boy gazed with frightened look.

"Don't beat me, Mother Watson," he said, imploringly.

"I'll beat the laziness out of you," said the woman, vindictively. "See if I don't."

She clutched Mark by the collar, and was about to bring the strap down forcibly upon his back, ill protected by his thin jacket, when a visitor entered the room.

"What's the matter, Mrs. Watson?" asked the intruder.

"Oh, it's you, Mrs. Flanagan?" said the woman, holding the strap suspended in the air. "I'll tell you what's the matter. This little thief has come home, after selling only three boxes of matches the whole day, and I find he's stole a penny to buy an apple with. It's for that I'm goin' to beat him."

"Oh, let him alone, the poor lad," said Mrs. Flanagan, who was a warm-hearted Irish woman. "Maybe he was hungry."

"Then why didn't he work? Them that work can eat."

"Maybe people didn't want to buy."

"Well, I can't afford to keep him in his idleness," said Mrs. Watson. "He may go to bed without his supper."

"If he can't sell his matches, maybe people would give him something."

Mrs. Watson evidently thought favorably of this suggestion, for, turning to Mark, she said, "Go out again, you little thief, and mind you don't come in again till you've got twenty-five cents to bring to me. Do you mind that?"

Mark listened, but stood irresolute.

"I don't like to beg," he said.

"Don't like to beg!" screamed Mrs. Watson. "Do you mind that, now, Mrs. Flanagan? He's too proud to beg."

"Mother told me never to beg if I could help it," said Mark.

"Well, you can't help it," said the woman, flourishing the strap in a threatening manner. "Do you see this?"

"Yes."

"Well, you'll feel it too, if you don't do as I tell you. Go out now."

"I'm so hungry," said Mark; "won't you give me a piece of bread?"

"Not a mouthful till you bring back twenty-five cents. Start now, or you'll feel the strap."

The boy left the room with a slow step, and wearily descended the stairs. I hope my young readers will never know the hungry craving after food which tormented the poor little boy as he made made his way towards the street. But he had hardly reached the foot of the first staircase when he heard a low voice behind him, and, turning, beheld Mrs. Flanagan, who had hastily followed after him.

"Are you very hungry?" she asked.

"Yes, I'm faint with hunger."

"Poor boy!" she said, compassionately; "come in here a minute."

She opened the door of her own room which was just at the foot of the staircase, and gently pushed him in.

It was a room of the same general appearance as the one above, but was much neater looking.

"Biddy Flanagan isn't the woman to let a poor

motherless child go hungry when she's a bit of bread or meat by her. Here, Mark, lad, sit down, and I'll soon bring you something that'll warm up your poor stomach."

She opened a cupboard, and brought out a plate containing a small quantity of cold beef, and two slices of bread.

"There's some better mate than you'll get of Mother Watson. It's cold, but it's good."

"She never gives me any meat at all," said Mark. gazing with a look of eager anticipation at the plate which to his famished eye looked so inviting.

"I'll be bound she don't," said Mrs. Flanagan. "Talk of you being lazy! What does she do herself but sit all day doing nothin' except drink whiskey from the black bottle! She might get washin' to do, as I do, if she wanted to, but she won't work. She expects you to get money enough for both of you."

Meanwhile Mrs. Flanagan had poured out a cup of tea from an old tin teapot that stood on the stove.

"There, drink that, Mark dear," she said. "It'll arm you up, and you'll need it this cold night, I'm thinkin'."

The tea was not of the best quality, and the cup was cracked and discolored; but to Mark it was grateful and refreshing, and he eagerly drank it.

"Is it good?" asked the sympathizing woman, observing with satisfaction the eagerness with which it was drunk.

"Yes, it makes me feel warm," said Mark.

"It's better nor the whiskey Mother Watson drinks," said Mrs. Flanagan. "It won't make your nose red like hers. It would be a sight better for her if she'd throw away the whiskey, and take to the tea."

"You are very kind, Mrs. Flanagan," said Mark, rising from the table, feeling fifty per cent. better than when he sat down.

"Oh bother now, don't say a word about it! Shure you're welcome to the bit you've eaten, and the little sup of tea. Come in again when you feel hungry, and Bridget Flanagan won't be the woman to send you off hungry if she's got anything in the cupboard."

"I wish Mother Watson was as good as you are," said Mark.

"I aint so good as I might be," said Mrs. Flanagan; "but I wouldn't be guilty of tratin' a poor boy as that woman trates you, more shame to her! How came you with her any way? She aint your mother, is she."

"No," said Mark, shuddering at the bare idea. "My mother was a good woman, and worked hard. She didn't drink whiskey. Mother was always kind to me. I wish she was alive now."

"When did she die, Mark dear?"

"It's going on a year since she died. I didn't know what to do, but Mother Watson told me to come and live with her, and she'd take care of me."

"Sorra a bit of kindness there was in that," commented Mrs. Flanagan. "She wanted you to take care of her. Well, and what did she make you do?"

"She sent me out to earn what I could. Sometimes I would run on errands, but lately I have sold matches."

"Is it hard work sellin' them?"

"Sometimes I do pretty well, but some days it seems as if nobody wanted any. To-day I went round to a great many offices, but they all had as many as they wanted, and I didn't sell but three boxes. I tried to sell more, indeed I did, but I couldn't."

"No doubt you did, Mark, dear. It's cold you must be in that thin jacket of yours this cold weather. I've got a shawl you may wear if you like. You'll not lose it, I know."

But Mark had a boy's natural dislike to being dressed as a girl, knowing, moreover, that his appear ance in the street with Mrs. Flanagan's shawl would subject him to the jeers of the street boys. So he declined the offer with thanks, and, buttoning up his thin jacket, descended the remaining staircase, and went out again into the chilling and uninviting street. A chilly, drizzling rain had just set in, and this made it even more dreary than it had been during the day.

CHAPTER VI.

BEN GIBSON.

BUT it was not so much the storm or the cold weather that Mark cared for. He had become used to these, so far as one can become used to what is very disagreeable. If after a hard day's work he had had a good home to come back to, or a kind and sympathizing friend, he would have had that thought to cheer him up. But Mother Watson cared nothing for him, except for the money he brought her, and Mark found it impossible either to cherish love or respect for the coarse woman whom he generally found more or less affected by whiskey.

Cold and hungry as he had been oftentimes, he had always shrunk from begging. It seemed to lower him in his own thoughts to ask charity of others. Mother Watson had suggested it to him once or twice, but had never actually commanded it before. Now he was required to bring home twenty-five cents. He

DICK AS A PHILANTHROPIST.

knew very well what would be the result if he failed to do this. Mother Watson would apply the leather strap with merciless fury, and he knew that his strength was as nothing compared to hers. So, for the first time in his life, he felt that he must make up his mind to beg.

He retraced his steps to the head of Frankfort Street, and walked slowly down Nassau Street. The rain was falling, as I have said, and those who could remained under shelter. Besides, business hours were over. The thousands who during the day made the lower part of the city a busy hive had gone to their homes in the upper portion of the island, or across the river to Brooklyn or the towns on the Jersey shore. So, however willing he might be to beg, there did not seem to be much chance at present.

The rain increased, and Mark in his thin clothes was soon drenched to the skin. He felt damp, cold, and uncomfortable. But there was no rest for him. The only home he had was shut to him, unless he should bring home twenty five-cents, and of this there seemed very little prospect.

At the corner of Fulton Street he fell in with a

boy of twelve, short and sturdy in frame, dressed in a coat whose tails nearly reached the sidewalk. Though scarcely in the fashion, it was warmer than Mark's, and the proprietor troubled himself very little about the looks.

This boy, whom Mark recognized as Ben Gibson, had a clay pipe in his mouth, which he seemed to be smoking with evident enjoyment.

"Where you goin'?" he asked, halting in front of Mark.

"I don't know," said Mark.

"Don't know!" repeated Ben, taking his pipe from his mouth, and spitting. "Where's your matches?"

"I left them at home."

"Then what'd did you come out for in this storm?"

"The woman I live with won't let me come home till I've brought her twenty-five cents."

"How'd you expect to get it?"

"She wants me to beg."

"That's a good way," said Ben, approvingly; "when you get hold of a soft chap, or a lady Them s the ones to shell out."

"I don't like it," said Mark. "I don't want people to think me a beggar."

"What's the odds?" said Ben, philosophically. "You're just the chap to make a good beggar."

"What do you mean by that, Ben?" said Mark, who was far from considering this much of a compliment.

"Why you're a thin, pale little chap, that people will pity easy. Now I aint the right cut for a beggar. I tried it once, but it was no go."

"Why not?" asked Mark, who began to be interested in spite of himself.

"You see," said Ben, again puffing out a volume of smoke, "I look too tough, as if I could take care of myself. People don't pity me. I tried it one night when I was hard up. I hadn't got but six cents, and I wanted to go to the Old Bowery bad. So I went up to a gent as was comin' up Wall Street from the Ferry, and said, 'Won't you give a poor boy a few pennies to save him from starvin'?'

"'So you're almost starvin', are you, my lad?' says he.

"'Yes, sir,' says I, as faint as I could.

"'Well, starvin' seems to agree with you,' says

he, laughin'. 'You're the healthiest-lookin' beggar I've seen in a good while.'

"I tried it again on another gent, and he told me he guessed I was lazy; that a good stout boy like me ought to work. So I didn't make much beggin', and had to give up goin' to the Old Bowery that night, which I was precious sorry for, for there was a great benefit that evenin'. Been there often?"

"No, I never went."

"Never went to the Old Bowery!" ejaculated Ben, whistling in his amazement. "Where were you raised, I'd like to know? I should think you was a country greeny, I should."

"I never had a chance," said Mark, who began to feel a little ashamed of the confession.

"Won't your old woman let you go?"

"I never have any money to go."

"If I was flush I'd take you myself. It's only fifteen cents," said Ben. "But I haven't got money enough only for one ticket. I'm goin' to-night."

"Are you?" asked Mark, a little enviously.

"Yes, it's a good way to pass a rainy evenin'. You've got a warm room to be in, let alone the play, which is splendid. Now, if you could only beg fifteen cents from some charitable cove, you might go along of me."

"If I get any money I've got to carry it home."

"Suppose you don't, will the old woman cut up rough?"

"She'll beat me with a strap," said Mark, shuddering.

'What makes you let her do it?" demanded Ben, rather disdainfully.

"I can't help it."

"She wouldn't beat me," said Ben, decidedly.

"What would you do?" asked Mark, with interest.

"What would I do?" retorted Ben. "I'd kick, and bite, and give her one for herself between the eyes. That's what I'd do. She'd find me a hard case, I reckon."

"It wouldn't be any use for me to try that," said Mark. "She's too strong."

"It don't take much to handle you," said Ben, taking a critical survey of the physical points of Mark. "You're most light enough to blow away."

"I'm only ten years old," said Mark, apologetically. "I shall be bigger some time."

"Maybe," said Ben. dubiously; "but you don't look as if you'd ever be tough like me."

"There," he added, after a pause, "I've smoked all my 'baccy. I wish I'd got some more."

"Do you like to smoke?" asked Mark.

"It warms a feller up," said Ben. "It's jest the thing for a cold, wet day like this. Didn't you ever try it?"

"No."

"If I'd got some 'baccy here, I'd give you a whiff; but I think it would make you sick the first time."

"I don't think I should like it," said Mark, who had never felt any desire to smoke, though he knew plenty of boys who indulged in the habit.

"That's because you don't know nothin' about it," remarked Ben. "I didn't like it at first till I got learned."

"Do you smoke often?"

"Every day after I get through blackin' boots; that is, when I ain't hard up, and can't raise the stamps to pay for the 'baccy. But I guess I'll be goin' up to the Old Bowery. It's most time for the doors to open. Where you goin'?"

"I don't know where to go," said Mark, helplessly.

"I'll tell you where you'd better go. You won' find nobody round here. Besides it aint comfortable lettin' the rain fall on you and wet you through." (While this conversation was going on, the boys had sheltered themselves in a doorway.) "Just you go down to Fulton Market. There you'll be out of the wet, and you'll see plenty of people passin' through when the boats come in. Maybe some of 'em will give you somethin'. Then ag'in, there's the boats. Some nights I sleep aboard the boats."

"You do? Will they let you?"

"They don't notice. I just pay my two cents, and go aboard, and snuggle up in a corner and go to sleep. So I ride to Brooklyn and back all night. That's cheaper'n the Newsboys' Lodgin' House, for it only costs two cents. One night a gentleman came to me, and woke me up, and said, 'We've got to Brooklyn, my lad. If you don't get up they'll carry you back again.'

"I jumped up and told him I was much obliged, as I didn't know what my family would say if I didn't get home by eleven o'clock. Then, just as soon as his back was turned, I sat down again and went to sleep. It aint so bad sleepin' aboard the boat, 'specially in a cold night. They keep the cabin warm, and though the seat isn't partic'larly soft its better'n bein' out in the street. If you don't get your twenty-five cents, and are afraid of a lickin', you'd better sleep aboard the boat."

"Perhaps I will," said Mark, to whom the idea was not unwelcome, for it would at all events save him for that night from the beating which would be his portion if he came home without the required sum.

"Well, good-night," said Ben; "I'll be goin' along."

"Good-night, Ben," said Mark, "I guess I'll go to Fulton Market."

Accordingly Mark turned down Fulton Street, while Ben steered in the direction of Chatham Street, through which it was necessary to pass in order to reach the theatre, which is situated on the Bowery, not far from its junction with Chatham Street.

Ben Gibson is a type of a numerous class of improvident boys, who live on from day to day, careless of appearances, spending their evenings where they can, at the theatre when their means admit, and sometimes at gambling saloons. Not naturally bad, they drift into bad habits from the force of outward circumstances. They early learn to smoke or chew, finding in tobacco some comfort during the cold and wet days, either ignorant of or indifferent to the harm which the insidious weed will do to their constitutions. So their growth is checked, or their blood is impoverished, as is shown by their pale faces.

As for Ben, he was gifted with a sturdy frame and an excellent constitution, and appeared as yet to exhibit none of the baneful effects of this habit. But no growing boy can smoke without ultimately being affected by it, and such will no doubt be the case with Ben.

CHAPTER VII.

FULTON MARKET.

JUST across from Fulton Ferry stands Fulton Market. It is nearly fifty years old, having been built in 1821, on ground formerly occupied by unsightly wooden buildings, which were, perhaps fortunately, swept away by fire. It covers the block bounded by Fulton, South, Beekman, and Front Streets, and was erected at a cost of about quarter of a million of dollars.

This is the chief of the great city markets, and an immense business is done here. There is hardly an hour in the twenty-four in which there is an entire lull in the business of the place. Some of the outside shops and booths are kept open all night, while the supplies of fish, meats, and vegetables for the market proper are brought at a very early hour, almost before it can be called morning.

Besides the market proper the surrounding sidewalks are roofed over, and lined with sheps and booths of the most diverse character, at which almost every conceivable article can be purchased. Most numerous, perhaps, are the chief restaurants, the counters loaded with cakes and pies, with a steaming vessel of coffee smoking at one end. The floors are sanded, and the accommodations are far from elegant or luxurious ; but it is said that the viands are by no means to be despised. Then there are fruit-stalls with tempting heaps of oranges, apples, and in their season the fruits of summer, presided over for the most part by old women, who scan shrewdly the faces of passers-by, and are ready on the smallest provocation to vaunt the merits of their wares. There are candy and cocoa-nut cakes for those who have a sweet tooth, and many a shop-boy invests in these on his way to or from Brooklyn to the New York store where he is employed; or the father of a family, on his way to his Brooklyn home, thinks of the little ones awaiting him, and indulges in a purchase of what he knows will be sure to be acceptable to them.

But it is not only the wants of the body that are provided for at Fulton Market. On the Fulton Street side may be found extensive booths, at which are displayed for sale a tempting array of papers, mag azines, and books, as well as stationery, photograph albums, etc., generally at prices twenty or thirty per cent. lower than is demanded for them in the more pretentious Broadway or Fulton Avenue stores.

Even at night, therefore, the outer portion of the market presents a bright and cheerful shelter from the inclement weather, being securely roofed over, and well lighted, while some of the booths are kept open, however late the hour.

Ben Gibson, therefore, was right in directing Mark to Fulton Market, as probably the most comfortable place to be found in the pouring rain which made the thoroughfares dismal and dreary. Mark, of course, had been in Fulton Market often, and saw at once the wisdom of the advice. He ran down Fulton Street as fast as he could, and arrived there panting and wet to the skin. Uncomfortable as he was, the change from the wet streets to the bright and com paratively warm shelter of the market made him at once more cheerful. In fact, it compared favorably with the cold and uninviting room which he shared with Mother Watson.

As Mark looked around him, he could not help

wishing that he tended in one of the little restaurants that looked so bright and inviting to him. Those who are accustomed to lunch at Delmonico's, or at some of the large and stylish hotels, or have their meals served by attentive servants in brown stone dwellings in the more fashionable quarters of the city, would be likely to turn up their noses at his humble taste, and would feel it an infliction to take a meal amid such plebeian surroundings. But then Mark knew nothing about the fare at Delmonico's, and was far enough from living in a brown stone front, and so his ideas of happiness and luxury were not very exalted, or he would scarcely have envied a stout butcher boy whom he saw sitting at an unpainted wooden table, partaking of a repast which was more abundant than choice.

But from the surrounding comfort Mark's thoughts were brought back to the disagreeable business which brought him here. He was to solicit charity from some one of the passers-by, and with a sigh he began to look about him to select some compassionate face.

"If there was only somebody here that wanted an errand done," he thought, "and would pay me twenty-five cents for doing it, I wouldn't have to beg

I'd rather work two hours for the money than beg it."

But there seemed little chance of this. In the busy portion of the day there might have been some chance, though this would be uncertain; but now it was very improbable. If he wanted to get twenty-five cents that night he must get it from charity.

A beginning must be made, however disagreeable. So Mark went up to a young man who was passing along on his way to the boat, and in a shamefaced manner said, "Will you give me a few pennies, please?"

The young man looked good-natured, and it was that which gave Mark confidence to address him.

"You want some pennies, do you?" he said, with a smile, pausing in his walk.

"If you please, sir."

"I suppose your wife and family are starving, eh?"

"I haven't got any wife or family, sir," said Mark.

"But you've got a sick mother, or some brothers or sisters that are starving, haven't you?"

"No, sir."

"Then I'm afraid you're not up to your business How long have you been round begging?"

"Never before," said Mark, rather indignantly.

"Ah, that accounts for it. You haven't learned the business yet. After a few weeks you'll have a sick mother starving at home. They all do, you know."

"My mother is dead," said Mark; "I shan't tell a lie to get money."

"Come. you're rather a remarkable boy," said the young man, who was a reporter on a daily paper, going over to attend a meeting in Brooklyn, to write an account of it to appear in one of the city dailies in the morning. "I don't generally give money in such cases, but I must make an exception in your case."

He drew a dime from his vest-pocket and handed it to Mark.

Mark took it with a blush of mortification at the necessity.

"I wouldn't beg if I could help it," he said, desiring to justify himself in the eyes of the good-natured young man.

"I'm glad to hear that. Johnny." (Johnny is a

common name applied to boys whose names are unknown.) "It isn't a very creditable business. What makes you beg, then?"

"I shall be beaten if I don't," said Mark.

"That's bad. Who will beat you?"

"Mother Watson."

"Tell Mother Watson, with my compliments, that she's a wicked old tyrant. I'll tell you what, my lad, you must grow as fast as you can, and by and by you'll get too large for that motherly old woman to whip. But there goes the bell. I must be getting aboard."

This was the result of Mark's first begging appeal. He looked at the money, and wished he had got it in any other way. If it had been the reward of an hour's work he would have gazed at it with much greater satisfaction.

Well, he had made a beginning. He had got ten cents. But there still remained fifteen cents to obtain, and without that he did not feel safe in going back.

So he looked about him for another person to address. This time he thought he would ask a lady. Accordingly he went up to one, who was walking with her son, a boy of sixteen, to judge from appearance, and asked for a few pennies.

"Get out of my way, you little beggar!" she said, in a disagreeable tone. "Aint you ashamed of yourself, going round begging, instead of earning money like honest people?"

"I've been trying to earn money all day," said Mark, rather indignant at this attack.

"Oh no doubt," sneered the woman. "I don't think you'll hurt yourself with work."

"I was round the streets all day trying to sell matches," said Mark.

"You mustn't believe what he says, mother," said the boy. "They're all a set of humbugs, and will lie as fast as they can talk."

"I've no doubt of it, Roswell," said Mrs. Crawford. "Such little impostors never get anything out of me. I've got other uses for my money."

Mark was a gentle, peaceful boy, but such attacks naturally made him indignant.

"I am not an impostor, and I neither lie nor steal," he said, looking alternately from the mother tc the son.

"Oh, you're a fine young man. I've no doubt,"

said Roswell, with a sneer. "But we'd better be getting on, mother, unless you mean to stop in Fulton Market all night."

So mother and son passed on, leaving Mark with a sense of mortification and injury. He would have given the ten cents he had, not to have asked charity of this woman who had answered him so unpleasantly.

Those of my readers who have read the two preceding volumes of this series will recognize in Roswell Crawford and his mother old acquaintances who played an important part in the former stories. As, however, I may have some new readers, it may be as well to explain that Roswell was a self-conceited boy, who prided himself on being "the son of a gentleman," and whose great desire was to find a place where the pay would be large and the duties very small. Unfortunately for his pride, his father had failed in business shortly before he died, and his mother had been compelled to keep a boarding-house. She, too, was troubled with a pride very similar to that of her son, and chafed inwardly at her position, instead of reconciling herself to it, as many better persons have done

Roswell was not very fortunate in retaining the positions he obtained, being generally averse to doing anything except what he was absolutely obliged to do. He had lost a situation in a dry-goods store in Sixth Avenue, because he objected to carrying bundles, considering it beneath the dignity of a gentleman's son. Some months before he had tried to get Richard Hunter discharged from his situation in the hope of succeeding him in it; but this plot proved utterly unsuccessful, as is fully described in "Fame and Fortune."

We shall have more to do with Roswell Crawford in the course of the present story. At present he was employed in a retail bookstore up town, on a salary of six dollars a week.

CHAPTER VIII

ON THE FERRY-BOAT.

MARK had made two applications for charity, and still had but ten cents. The manner in which Mrs. Crawford met his appeal made the business seem more disagreeable than ever. Besides, he was getting tired. It was not more than eight o'clock, but he had been up early, and had been on his feet all day. He leaned against one of the stalls, but in so doing he aroused the suspicions of the vigilant old woman who presided over it.

"Just stand away there," she said. "You're watchin' for a chance to steal one of them apples."

"No, I'm not," said Mark, indignantly. "I never steal."

"Don't tell me," said the old woman, who had a hearty aversion to boys, some of whom, it must be confessed, had in times past played mean tricks on ner; "don't tell me! Them that beg will steal, and I see you beggin' just now."

To this Mark had no reply to make. He saw that he was already classed with the young street beggars, many of whom, as the old woman implied, had no particular objection to stealing, if they got a chance. Altogether he was so disgusted with his new business, that he felt it impossible for him to beg any more that night. But then came up the consideration that this would prevent his returning home. He very well knew what kind of a reception Mother Watson would give him, and he had a very unpleasant recollection and terror of the leather strap.

But where should he go? He must pass the night somewhere, and he already felt drowsy. Why should he not follow Ben Gibson's suggestions, and sleep on the Fulton ferry-boat? It would only cost two cents to get on board, and he might ride all night. Fortunately he had more than money enough for that, though he did not like to think how he came by the ten cents.

When Mark had made up his mind, he passed out of one of the entrances of the market, and, crossing the street, presented his ten cents at the wicket, where stood the fare-taker.

Without a look towards him, that functionary took the money, and pushed back eight cents. These Mark took, and passed round into the large room of the ferry-house.

The boat was not in, but he already saw it half-way across the river, speeding towards its pier.

There were a few persons waiting besides himself, but the great rush of travel was diminished for a short time. It would set in again about eleven o'clock when those who had passed the evening at some place of amusement in New York would be on their way home.

Mark with the rest waited till the boat reached its wharf. There was the usual bump, then the chain rattled, the wheel went round, and the passengers began to pour out upon the wharf. Mark passed into the boat, and went at once to the "gentlemen's cabin," situated on the left-hand side of the boat. Generally, however, gentlemen rather unfairly crowd into the ladies' cabin, sometimes compelling the ladies, to whom it of right belongs, to stand, while they complacently monopolize the seats. The gen tlemen's cabin, so called, is occupied by those who have a little more regard to the rights of ladies, and by the smokers, who are at liberty to indulge in their favorite comfort here.

When Mark entered, the air was redolent with tobacco-smoke, generally emitted from clay pipes and cheap cigars, and therefore not so agreeable as under other circumstances it might have been. But it was warm and comfortable, and that was a good deal.

In the corner Mark espied a wide seat nearly double the size of an ordinary seat, and this he decided would make the most comfortable niche for him.

He settled himself down there as well as he could. The seat was hard, and not so comfortable as it might have been; but then Mark was not accustomed to beds of down, and he was so weary that his eyes closed and he was soon in the land of dreams.

He was dimly conscious of the arrival at the Brooklyn side, and the ensuing hurried exit of passengers from that part of the cabin in which he was, but it was only a slight interruption, and when the boat, having set out on its homeward trip, reached the New York side, he was fast asleep.

"Poor little fellow!" thought more than one, with a hasty glance at the sleeping boy. "He is taking his comfort where he can."

But there was no good Samaritan to take him by the hand, and inquire into his hardships, and provide for his necessities, or rather there was one, and that one well known to us.

Richard Hunter and his friend Henry Fosdick had been to Brooklyn that evening to attend an instructive lecture which they had seen announced in one of the daily papers. The lecture concluded at half-past nine, and they took the ten o'clock boat over the Fulton ferry.

They seated themselves in the first cabin, towards the Brooklyn side, and did not, therefore, see Mark until they passed through the other cabin on the arrival of the boat at New York.

"Look there, Fosdick," said Richard Hunter. "See that poor little chap asleep in the corner. Doesn't it remind you of the times we used to have, when we were as badly off as he?"

"Yes, Dick, but I don't think I ever slept on a ferry-boat."

"That's because you were not on the streets long

I took care of myself eight years, and more than once took a cheap bed for two cents on a boat like this. Most likely I've slept in that very corner."

"It was a hard life, Dick."

"Yes, and a hard bed too; but there's a good many that are no better off now. I always feel like doing something to help along those like this little chap here."

"I wonder what he is, — a boot-black?"

"He hasn't got any brush or box with him. Perhaps he's a newsboy. I think I'll give him a surprise."

"Wake him up, do you mean?"

"No, poor little chap! Let him sleep. I'll put fifty cents in his pocket, and when he wakes up he won't know where it came from."

"That's a good idea, Dick. I'll do the same. All right."

"Here's the money. Put mine in with yours. Don't wake him up."

Dick walked softly up to the match-boy, and gently inserted the money — one dollar — in one of the pockets of his ragged vest

Mark was so fast asleep that he was entirely unconscious of the benevolent act.

"That'll make him open his eyes in the morning," he said.

"Unless somebody relieves him of the money during his sleep."

"Not much chance of that. Pickpockets won't be very apt to meddle with such a ragged little chap as that, unless it's in a fit of temporary aberration of mind."

"You're right, Dick. But we must hurry out now, or we shall be carried back to Brooklyn."

"And so get more than our money's worth. I wouldn't want to cheat the corporation so extensively as that."

So the two friends passed out of the boat, and left the match boy asleep in the cabin, quite unconscious that good fortune had hovered over him, and made him richer by a dollar, while he slept.

While we are waiting for him to awake, we may as well follow Richard Hunter and his friend home.

Fosdick's good fortune, which we recorded in the earlier chapters of this volume had made no particular change in their arrangements. They were already living in better style than was usual among youths situated as they were. There was this difference, however, that whereas formerly Dick paid the greater part of the joint expense it was now divided equally. It will be remembered that Fosdick's interest on the twenty bank shares purchased in his name amounted to one hundred and sixty dollars annually, and this just about enabled him to pay his own way, though not leaving him a large surplus for clothing and incidental expenses. It could not be long, however, before his pay would be increased at the store, probably by two dollars a week. Until that time he could economize a little; for upon one thing he had made up his mind, — not to trench upon his principal except in case of sickness or absolute necessity.

The boys had not forgotten or neglected the commission which they had undertaken for Mr. Hiram Bates. They had visited, on the evening after he left, the Newsboys' Lodging House, then located at the corner of Fulton and Nassau Streets, in the upper part of the "Sun" building, and had consulted Mr. O'Connor, the efficient superintendent, as to the boy of whom they were in search. But he had no information to supply them with. He promised to inquire among the boys who frequented the lodge, as it was possible that there might be some among them who might have fallen in with a boy named Talbot.

Richard Hunter also sought out some of his old acquaintances, who were still engaged in blacking boots, or selling newspapers, and offered a reward of five dollars for the discovery of a boy of ten, named Talbot, or John Talbot.

As the result of this offer a red-haired boy was brought round to the counting-room one day, who stoutly asserted that his name was John Talbot, and his guide in consequence claimed the reward. Dick, however, had considerable doubt as to the genuineness of this claim, and called the errand-boy, known to the readers of earlier volumes, as Micky Maguire.

"Micky," said Richard, "this boy says he is John Talbot. Do you know him?"

"Know him!" repeated Micky; "I've knowed him ever since he was so high. He's no more John Talbot than I am. His name is Tim Hogan, and I'll defy him to say it isn't."

Tim looked guilty, and his companion gave up the attempt to obtain the promised reward. He had hired Tim by the promise of a dollar to say he was John Talbot, hoping by the means to clear four dollars for himself.

"That boy'll rise to a seat in the Common Council if he lives long enough," said Dick. "He's an unusually promising specimen."

CHAPTER IX.

A PLEASANT DISCOVERY.

The night wore away, and still Mark, the match boy, continued to sleep soundly in the corner of the cabin where he had established himself. One of the boat hands passing through noticed him, and was on the point of waking him, but, observing his weary look and thin attire, refrained from an impulse of compassion. He had a boy of about the same age, and the thought came to him that some time his boy might be placed in the same situation, and this warmed his heart towards the little vagrant.

"I suppose I ought to wake him up," he reflected, "but he isn't doing any harm there, and he may as well have his sleep out."

So Mark slept on, — a merciful sleep, in which he forgot his poverty and friendless condition; a sleep which brought new strength and refreshment to his limbs.

When he woke up it was six o'clock in the morning. But it was quite dark still, for it was in December, and, so far as appearances went, it might have been midnight. But already sleepy men and boys were on their way to the great city to their daily work. Some were employed a considerable distance up town, and must be at their posts at seven. Others were employed in the markets and must be stirring at an early hour. There were keepers of street-stands, who liked to be ready for the first wave in the tide of daily travel that was to sweep without interruption through the city streets until late at night. So, altogether, even at this early hour there was quite a number of passengers.

Mark rubbed his eyes, not quite sure where he was, or how he got there. He half expected to hear the harsh voice of Mother Watson, which usually aroused him to his daily toil. But there was no Mother Watson to be seen, only sleepy, gaping men and boys, clad in working dresses.

Mark sat up and looked around him.

"Well, young chap, you've had a nap, haven't you?" said a man at his side, who appeared, from a strong smell of paint about his clothes, to be a journeyman painter.

"Yes," said Mark. "Is it morning?"

"To be sure it is. What did you expect it was?"

"Then I've been sleeping all night," said the match boy, in surprise.

"Where?"

"Here."

"In that corner?" asked the painter.

"Yes," said Mark; "I came aboard last night, and fell asleep, and that's the last I remember."

"It must be rather hard to the bones," said the painter. "I think that I should prefer a regular bed."

"I do feel rather sore," said the match boy; "but I slept bully."

"A little chap like you can curl up anywhere. I don't think I could sleep very well on these seats. Haven't you got any home?"

"Yes," said Mark, "a sort of a home."

"Then why didn't you sleep at home?"

"I knew I should get a beating if I went home without twenty-five cents."

"Well, that's hard luck. I wonder how I should feel," he continued, laughing, "if my wife gave me a beating when I came home short of funds."

But here the usual bump indicated the arrival of the boat at the slip, and all the passengers, the painter included, rose, and hurried to the edge of the boat.

With the rest went Mark. He had no particular object in going thus early; but his sleep was over. and there was no inducement to remain longer in the boat.

The rain was over also. The streets were still wet from the effects of the quantity that had fallen, but there was no prospect of any more. Mark's wet clothes had dried in the warm, dry atmosphere of the cabin, and he felt considerably better than on the evening previous.

Now, however, he could not help wondering what Mother Watson had thought of his absence.

"She'll be mad, I know," he thought. "I suppose she'll whip me when I get back."

This certainly was not a pleasant thought. The

leather strap was an old enemy of his which he dreaded, and with good reason. He was afraid that he would get a more severe beating, for not having returned the night before, at the hands of the angry old woman.

"I wish I didn't live with Mother Watson," he thought.

Straight upon this thought came another. "Why should he?"

Mother Watson had no claim upon him. Upon his mother's death she had assumed the charge of him, but, as it turned out, rather for her own advantage than his. She had taken all his earnings, and given him in return a share of her miserable apartment, a crust of bread or two, daily seasoned with occasional assaults with the leather strap. It had never occurred to Mark before, but now for the first time it dawned upon him that he had the worst of the bargain. He could live more comfortably by retaining his earnings, and spending them upon himself.

Mark was rather a timid, mild-mannered boy, or he would sooner have rebelled against the tyranny and abuse of Mother Watson. But he had had lit tle confidence in himself, and wanted somebody to lean on. In selecting the old woman, who had acted thus far as his guardian, he had leaned upon a broken reed. The last night's experience gave him a little courage. He reflected that he could sleep in the Newsboys' Lodging House for five cents, or on the ferry-boat again for two, while the fare at his old home was hardly so sumptuous but that he could obtain the same without very large expense.

So Mark thought seriously of breaking his yoke and declaring himself free and independent. A discovery which he made confirmed him in his half-formed resolution.

He remembered that after paying his toll he had eight cents left, which he had placed in his vest-pocket. He thought that these would enable him to get some breakfast, and drew them out. To his astonishment there were two silver half-dollars mingled with the coppers. Mark opened his eyes wide in astonishment. Where could they have come from? Was it possible that the tollman had given him them by mistake for pennies? That could not be, for two reasons: First, he remembered looking at the change as it was handed him, and he knew that there were no half-dollars among them. Again, the eight pennies were all there, the silver coins making the number ten.

It was certainly very strange and surprising, and puzzled Mark not a little. We, who know all about it, find the explanation very easy, but to the little match boy it was an unfathomable mystery.

The surprise, however, was of an agreeable character. With so much money in his possession, Mark felt like a man with a handsome balance at his banker's, and with the usual elasticity of youth he did not look forward to the time when this supply would be exhausted.

"I won't go back to Mother Watson," he determined. "She's beaten me times enough. I'll take care of myself."

While these thoughts were passing through his mind, he had walked up Fulton Street, and reached the corner of Nassau. Here he met his friend of the night before, Ben Gibson.

Ben looked rather sleepy. He had been at the Old Bowery Theatre the night before until twelve o'clock, and, having no money left to invest in a night's lodging, he had crept into a corner of the

"Times" printing office, and slept, but had not quite slept off his fatigue.

"Hallo, young 'un!" said he. "Where did you come from?"

"From Fulton Ferry," said Mark. "I slept on the boat."

"Did you? How'd you like it?"

"Pretty good," said Mark. "It was rather hard."

"How'd you make out begging?"

"Not very well. I got ten cents."

"So you didn't dare to go home to the old woman?"

"I shan't go home there any more," said the match boy.

"Do you mean it?"

"Yes, I do."

"Bully for you! I like your pluck. I wouldn't go back and get a licking, if I were you. What'll Mother Watson say?"

"She'll be mad, I expect," said Mark.

"Keep a sharp lookout for her. I'll tell you what you can do: stay near me, and if she comes prowlin' round I'll manage her."

"Could you?" said Mark, quickly, who, from certain recollections, had considerable fear of his stout tyrant

"You may just bet on that. What you goin' to do?"

"I think I shall go and get some breakfast," said Mark.

"So would I, if I had any tin; but I'm dead broke,— spent my last cent goin' to the Old Bowery. I'll have to wait till I've had one or two shines before I can eat breakfast."

"Are you hungry?"

"I'll bet I am."

"Because," said Mark, hesitating, "I'll lend you money enough for breakfast, and you can pay me when you earn it."

"You lend me money!" exclaimed Ben in astonishment. "Why, you haven't got but eight cents."

"Yes, I have," said Mark, producing the two half-dollars.

"Where'd you get them?" asked the boot-black in unfeigned surprise, looking at Mark as if he had all at once developed into an Astor or a Stewart.

"You haven't been begging this morning, have you?"

"No," said the match boy, "and I don't mean to beg again if I can help it."

"Then where'd you get the money?"

"I don't know"

"Don't know! You haven't been stealin', have you?"

Mark disclaimed the imputation indignantly.

"Then you found a pocket-book?"

"No, I didn't."

"Then where did you get the money?"

"I don't know any more than you do. When I went to sleep on the boat I didn't have it, but this morning when I felt in my pocket it was there."

"That's mighty queer," said Ben, whistling.

"So I think."

"It's good money, aint it?"

"Try it and see."

Ben tossed up one of the coins. It fell with a clear, ringing sound on the sidewalk.

"Yes, that's good," he said. "I just wish somebody'd treat me that way. Maybe it's the vest. If 'tis I'd like to buy it."

"I don't think it's that," said Mark, laughing

"Anyway you've got the money. I'll borrow twenty cents of you, and we'll go and get some breakfast."

CHAPTER X.

ON THE WAR PATH.

BEN led the way to a cheap restaurant, where for eighteen cents each of the boys got a breakfast, which to their not very fastidious tastes proved very satisfactory.

"There," said Ben, with a sigh of satisfaction, as they rose from the table, "now I feel like work; I'll pay up that money afore night."

"All right," said Mark.

"What are you goin' to do?"

"I don't know," said Mark, irresolutely.

"You're a match boy,—aint you?"

"Yes."

"Where's your matches?"

"In Mother Watson's room."

"You might go and get 'em when she's out."

"No," said Mark, shaking his head, "I won't do that."

"Why not? You aint afraid to go round there, be you?"

"It isn't that, — but the matches are hers, not mine."

"What's the odds?"

"I won't take anything of hers."

"Well, you can buy some of your own, then. You've got money enough."

"So I will," said Mark. "It's lucky that money came to me in my sleep."

"That's a lucky boat. I guess I'll go there and sleep to-night."

Mark did as he proposed. With the money he had he was able to purchase a good supply of matches, and when it became light enough he began to vend them.

Hitherto he had not been very fortunate in the disposal of his wares, being timid and bashful; but then he was working for Mother Watson, and expected to derive very little advantage for himself from his labors. Now he was working for himself, and this seemed to put new spirit and courage into him. Then again he felt that he had shaken off the hateful thraldom in which Mother Watson had held him, and this gave him a hopefulness which he had not before possessed.

The consequence was that at noon he found that he had earned forty cents in addition to his investment. At that time, too, Ben was ready to pay him his loan, so that Mark found himself twenty-two cents better off than he had been in the morning, having a capital of a dollar and thirty cents, out of which, however, he must purchase his dinner.

While he is getting on in such an encouraging manner we must go back to Mother Watson.

When Mark did not return the night before she grumbled considerably, but no thought of his intentional desertion dawned upon her. Indeed, she counted upon his timidity and lack of courage, knowing well that a more spirited boy would have broken her chain long before. She only thought, therefore, that he had not got the twenty-five cents, and did not dare to come back, especially as she had forbidden him to do so.

So, determining to give him a taste of the leather strap in the morning, she went to bed, first taking a fresh potation from the whiskey bottle, which was her constant companion.

Late in the morning Mother Watson woke, feeling as usual, at that hour of the day, cross and uncomfortable, and with a strong desire to make some one else uncomfortable. But Mark, whom she usually made to bear the burden of her temper, was still away. For the first time the old woman began to feel a little apprehensive that he had deserted her. This was far from suiting her, as she found his earnings very convenient, and found it besides pleasant to have somebody to scold.

She hastily dressed, without paying much attention to her toilet. Indeed to do Mother Watson justice, her mind was far from being filled with the vanity of dress, and if she erred on that subject it was in the opposite extreme.

When her simple toilet was accomplished she went downstairs, and knocked at Mrs. Flanagan's door.

"Come in!" said a hearty voice.

Mrs. Flanagan was hard at work at her wash-tub, and had been for a good couple of hours. She raised her good-natured face as the old woman entered.

"The top of the morning to you, Mother Watson," she said. "I hope you're in fine health this morning, mum."

"Then you'll be disappointed," said Mrs. Watson. "I've got a bad feeling at my stomach, and have it most every morning."

"It's the whiskey," thought Mrs. Flanagan; but she thought it best not to intimate as much, as it might lead to hostilities.

"Better take a cup of tea," said she.

"I haven't got any," said the old woman. "I wouldn't mind a sup if you've got some handy."

"Sit down then," said Mrs. Flanagan, hospitably. "I've got some left from breakfast, only it's cold, but if you'll wait a bit, I'll warm it over for you."

Nothing loth, Mother Watson sank into a chair, and began to give a full account of her ailments to her neighbor, who tried hard to sympathize with her, though, knowing the cause of the ailments, she found this rather difficult.

"Have you seen anything of my boy this morning?" she asked after a while.

"What, Mark?" said Mrs. Flanagan. "Didn't he come home last night?"

"No," said the old woman, "and he isn't home yet. When he does come I'll give him a dose of the strap. He's a bad, lazy, shiftless boy, and worries my life out."

"You're hard on the poor boy, Mother Watson. You must remember he's but a wisp of a lad, and hasn't much strength."

"He's strong enough," muttered Mother Watson. "It's lazy he is. Just let him come home, that's all!"

"You told him not to come home unless he had twenty-five cents to bring with him."

"So I did, and why didn't he do it?"

"He couldn't get the money, it's likely, and he's afraid of bein' bate."

"Well, he will be bate then, Mrs. Flanagan, you may be sure of that," said the old woman, diving her hand into her pocket to see that the strap was safe.

"Then you're a bad, cruel woman, to bate that poor motherless child," said Mrs. Flanagan, with spirit.

"Say that again, Mrs. Flanagan," ejaculated Mother Watson, irefully. "My hearin' isn't as good as it was, and maybe I didn't hear you right."

"No wonder your hearin' isn't good," said Mrs

Flanagan, who now broke bounds completely. "I shouldn't think you'd have any sense left with the whiskey you drink."

"Perhaps you mean to insult me," said the old woman, glaring at her hostess with one of the frowns which used to send terror to the heart of poor Mark.

"Take it as you please, mum," said Mrs. Flanagan, intrepidly. "I'm entirely willin'. I've been wanting to spake my mind a long while, and now I've spoke it."

Mother Watson clutched the end of the strap in her pocket, and eyed her hostess with a half wish that it would do to treat her as she had treated Mark so often; but Mrs. Flanagan with her strong arms and sturdy frame looked like an antagonist not very easily overcome, and Mrs. Watson forbore, though unwillingly.

Meanwhile the tea was beginning to emit quite a savory odor, and the wily old woman thought it best to change her tactics.

Accordingly she burst into tears, and, rocking backward and forward, declared that she was a miserable old woman, and hadn't a friend in the world, and succeeded in getting up such a display of misery that the soft heart of Mrs. Flanagan was touched. and she apologized for the unpleasant personal observations she had made, and hoped Mother Watson would take the tea.

To this Mother Watson finally agreed, and intimating that she was faint, Mrs. Flanagan made some toast for her, of which the cunning old woman partook with exceeding relish, notwithstanding her state of unhappiness.

"Come in any time, Mother Watson," said Mrs. Flanagan, "when you want a sip of tea, and I'll be glad to have you take some with me."

"Thank you, Mrs. Flanagan; maybe I'll look in once in a while. A sip of tea goes to the right spot when I feel bad at my stomach."

"Must you be goin', Mother Watson?"

"Yes," said the old woman; "I'm goin' out on a little walk, to see my sister that keeps a candy-stand by the Park railins. If Mark comes in, will you tell him he'll find the matches upstairs?"

This Mrs. Flanagan promised to do, and the old woman went downstairs, and into the street.

But she had not stated her object quite correctly. It was true that she had a sister, who was in the confectionery and apple line, presiding over one of the stalls beside the Park railings. But the two sisters were not on very good terms, chiefly because the candy merchant, who was more industrious and correct in her habits than her sister, declined to lend money to Mother Watson, — a refusal which led to a perfect coolness between them. It was not therefore to see her that the old woman went out. She wanted to find Mark. She did not mean to lose her hold upon him, if there was any chance of retaining it, and she therefore made up her mind to visit the places where he was commonly to be found, and, when found, to bring him home, by violence, if necessary.

So with an old plaid cloak depending from her broad shoulders, and her hand grasping the strap in her pocket, she made her way to the square, peering about on all sides with her ferret-like eyes in the hope of discovering the missing boy.

CHAPTER XI.

MARK'S VICTORY.

MEANWHILE Mark, rejoicing in his new-found freedom, had started on a business walk among the stores and offices at the lower part of Nassau Street, and among the law and banking offices of Wall Street. Fortunately for Mark there had been a rise in stocks, and Wall Street was in a good-humor. So a few of the crumbs from the tables of the prosperous bankers and brokers fell in his way. One man, who had just realized ten thousand dollars on a rise in some railway securities, handed Mark fifty cents, but declined to take any of his wares. So this was all clear profit and quite a windfall for the little match boy Again, in one or two cases he received double price for some of his matches, and the result was that he found himself by eleven o'clock the possessor of two dollars and a quarter, with a few boxes of matches still left.

Mark could hardly realize his own good fortune. Somehow it seemed a great deal more profitable as well as more agreeable to be in business for himself, than to be acting as the agent of Mother Watson. Mark determined that he would never go back to her unless he was actually obliged to do so.

He wanted somebody to sympathize with him in his good fortune, and, as he had nearly sold out, he determined to hunt up Ben Gibson, and inform him of his run of luck.

Ben, as he knew, was generally to be found on Nassau Street, somewhere near the corner of Spruce Street. He therefore turned up Nassau Street from Wall, and in five minutes he reached the business stand of his friend Ben.

Ben had just finished up a job as Mark came up. His patron was a young man of verdant appearance, who, it was quite evident, hailed from the country. He wore a blue coat with brass buttons, and a tall hat in the style of ten years before, with an immense top. He gazed with complacency at the fine polish which Ben had imparted to his boots, — a pair of stout cowhides, — and inquired with an assumption of indifference: —

"Well, boy, what's the tax?"

"Twenty-five cents," said Ben, coolly.

"Twenty-five cents!" ejaculated the customer, with a gasp of amazement. "Come now, you're jokin'."

"No, I aint," said Ben.

"You don't mean to say you charge twenty-five cents for five minutes' work?"

"Reg'lar price," said Ben.

"Why I don't get but twelve and a half cents an hour when I work out hayin'," said the young man in a tone expressive of his sense of the unfairness of the comparative compensation.

"Maybe you don't have to pay a big license," said Ben.

"A license for blackin' boots?" ejaculated the countryman, in surprise.

"In course. I have to deposit five hundred dollars, more or less, in the city treasury, before I can black boots."

"Five—hundred—dollars!" repeated the customer, opening his eyes wide at the information.

"In course," said Ben. "If I didn't they'd put me in jail for a year."

"And does he pay a license too?" asked the countryman, pointing to Mark, who had just come up.

"He only has to pay two hundred and fifty dollars." said Ben. "They aint so hard on him as on us."

The young man drew out his wallet reluctantly, and managed to raise twenty-three cents, which he handed to Ben.

"I wouldn't have had my boots blacked, if I'd known the price," he said. "I could have blacked 'em myself at home. They didn't cost but three dollars, and it don't pay to give twenty-five cents to have 'em blacked."

"It'll make 'em last twice as long," said Ben. "My blackin' is the superiorest kind, and keeps boots from wearin' out."

"I havn't got the other two cents," said the young man. "Aint that near enough?"

"It'll do," said Ben, magnanimously, "seein' you didn't know the price."

The victimized customer walked away, gratified to have saved the two cents, but hardly reconciled to have expended almost quarter of a dollar on a piece of work which he might have done himself before leaving home.

"Well, what luck, Mark?" said Ben. "I took in that chap neat, didn't I?"

"But you didn't tell the truth," said Mark. "You don't have to buy a license."

"Oh, what's the odds?" said Ben, whose ideas on the subject of truth were far from being strict. "It's all fair in business. Didn't that chap open his eyes when I told him about payin' five hundred dollars?"

"I don't think it's right, Ben," said Mark, seriously.

"Don't you go to preachin', Mark," said Ben, not altogether pleased. "You've been tied to an old woman's apron-string too long,—that's what's the matter with you."

"Mother Watson didn't teach me the truth," said Mark. "She don't care whether I tell it or not except to her. It was my mother that told me I ought always to tell the truth."

"Women don't know anything about business," said Ben. "Nobody in business speaks the truth. Do you see that sign?"

Mark looked across the street, and saw a large placard, setting forth that a stock of books and stationery was selling off at less than cost.

"Do you believe that?" asked Ben.

"Perhaps it's true," said Mark.

"Then you're jolly green, that's all I've got to say," said Ben. "But you haven't told me how much you've made."

"See here," said Mark, and he drew out his stock of money.

"Whew!" whistled Ben, in amazement. "You're in luck. I guess you've been speculatin' on your license too."

"No," said Mark; "one gentleman gave me fifty cents, and two others paid me double price."

"Why, you're gettin' rich!" said Ben. "Aint you glad you've left the old woman?"

But just then Mark lifted up his eyes, and saw a sight that blanched his cheek. There, bearing down upon him, and already but a few feet distant, was Mother Watson! She was getting over the ground as fast as her stoutness would allow. She had already caught sight of Mark, and her inflamed eyes were sparkling with triumphant joy. Mark saw with terror that her hand was already feeling in the pocket where she kept the leather strap. Much as he always feared the strap, the idea of having it applied to him in the public street made it even more distasteful.

"What shall I do, Ben?" he said, clutching the arm of his companion.

"What are you afraid of? Do you see a copp after you?"

A "copp" is the street-boy's name for a policeman.

"No," said Mark; "there's Mother Watson coming after me. Don't you see her?"

"That's Mother Watson, is it?" asked Ben, surveying the old body with a critical eye. "She's a beauty, she is!"

"What shall I do, Ben? She'll beat me."

"No, she won't," said Ben. "You just keep quiet, and leave her to me. Don't be afraid. She shan't touch you."

"She might strike you," said Mark, apprehensively.

"She'd better not!" said Ben, very decidedly; "not unless she wants to be landed in the middle of next week at very short notice."

By this time Mother Watson came up, puffing and panting with the extraordinary efforts she had made

She could not speak at first, but stood and glared at the match boy in a vindictive way.

"What's the matter with you, old lady?" asked Ben, coolly. "You aint took sick, be you? I'd offer to support your delicate form, but I'm afraid you'd be too much for me."

"What do you mean by runnin' away from home, you little thief?" said the old woman, at length regaining her breath. Of course her remark was addressed to Mark.

"You're very polite, old lady," said Ben; "but I've adopted that boy, and he's goin' to live with me now."

"I aint speakin' to you, you vagabone!" said Mother Watson, "so you needn't give me no more of your impertinence. I'm a-speakin' to him."

"I'm not going to live with you any more," said Mark, gaining a little courage from the coolness of his friend, the boot-black.

"Aint a goin' to live with me?" gasped the old woman, who could hardly believe she heard aright "Come right away, sir, or I'll drag you home."

"Don't you stir, Mark," said Ben.

Mother Watson drew out her strap, and tried to

get at the match boy, but Ben put himself persistently in her way.

"Clear out, you vagabone!" said the old lady, "or I'll give you something to make you quiet."

"You'd better keep quiet yourself," said Ben, not in the least frightened. "Don't you be afraid, Mark. If she kicks up a rumpus, I'll give her over to a copp. He'll settle her."

Mother Watson by this time was very much incensed. She pulled out her strap, and tried to get at Mark, but the boot-black foiled her efforts constantly.

Carried away with anger, she struck Ben with the strap.

"Look here, old lady," said Ben, "that's goin' a little too far. You won't use that strap again;" and with a dexterous and vigorous grasp he pulled it out of her hand.

"Give me that strap, you vagabone!" screamed the old woman, furiously.

"Look here, old lady, what are you up to?" demanded the voice of one having authority.

Mother Watson, turning round, saw an object for which she never had much partiality, — a policeman

"O sir," said she, bursting into maudlin tears, "it's my bad boy that I want to come home, and he won't come."

"Which is your boy,—that one?" asked the policeman, pointing to Ben Gibson.

"No, not that vagabone!" said the old woman, spitefully. "I wouldn't own him. It's that other boy."

"Do you belong to her?" asked the officer, addressing Mark.

"No, sir," said the match boy.

"He does," vociferated the old woman.

"Is he your son?"

"No," she said, after a moment's hesitation.

"Is he any relation of yours?"

"Yes, he's my nephew," said Mother Watson, making up her mind to a falsehood as the only means of recovering Mark.

"Is this true?" asked the officer.

"No, it isn't." said Mark. "She's no relation to me, but when my mother died she offered to take care of me. Instead of that she's half starved me, and beaten me with a strap when I didn't bring home as much money as she wanted."

"Then you don't want to go back with her?"

"No, I'm going to take care of myself."

"Is there anybody that will prove the truth of what you say?"

"Yes," said Mark, "I'll call Mrs. Flanagan."

"Who is she?"

"She lives in the same house with us."

"Shall he call her, or will you give him up?" asked the officer. "By the way, I think you're the same woman I saw drunk in the street last week."

Mother Watson took alarm at this remark, and, muttering that it was hard upon a poor widder woman to take her only nephew from her, shuffled off, leaving Mark and Ben in full possession of the field, with the terrible strap thrown in as a trophy of the victory they had won.

"I know her of old," said the policeman. "I guess youll do as well without her as with her."

Satisfied that there would be no more trouble, he resumed his walk, and Mark felt that now in truth be was free and independent.

As Mother Watson will not reappear in this story, it mav be said that only a fortnight later she was arrested for an assault upon her sister, the pro prietor of the apple-stand, from whom she had endeavored in vain to extort a loan, and was sentenced to the island for a period of three months, during which she ceased to grace metropolitan society.

CHAPTER XII.

THE NEWSBOYS' LODGING HOUSE.

WHEN Mother Watson had turned the corner, Mark breathed a sigh of relief.

"Don't you think she'll come back again?" he asked anxiously of Ben Gibson.

"No," said Ben, "she's scared of the copp. If she ever catches you alone, and tries to come any of her games, just call a copp, and she'll be in a hurry to leave."

"Well," said Mark, "I guess I'll try to sell the rest of my matches. I haven't got but a few."

"All right; I'll try for another shine, and then we'll go and have some dinner. I'd like to get hold of another greeny."

Mark started with his few remaining matches. The feeling that he was his own master, and had a little hoard of money for present expenses, gave him courage, and he was no longer deterred by his usual amidi y. In an hour he had succeeded in getting rid of ll his matches, and he was now the possessor of tw(dollars and seventy-five cents, including the money Ben Gibson owed him. Ben also was lucky enough to get two ten-cent customers, which helped his rec ipts by twenty cents. Ben, it may be re marked was not an advocate of the one-price system. He bla ked boots for five cents when he could get no more. When he thought there was a reasonable prospect of getting ten cents, that was his price. Sometimes, as in the case of the young man from the rural districts, he advanced his fee to twenty-five cents. I don't approve Ben's system for my part. I think it savors considerably of sharp practice, and that fair prices in the long run are the best for all parties.

The boys met again at one o'clock, and adjourned to a cheap underground restaurant on Nassau Street, where they obtained what seemed to them a luxurious meal of beefsteak, with a potato, a small plate of bread, and a cup of what went by the name of coffee. The steak was not quite up to the same article at Delmonico's, and there might be some reasonable doubts as to whether the coffee was a gen-nine article; but as neither of the boys knew the difference we may quote Ben's familiar phrase, and say, "What's the odds?"

Indeed, the free and easy manner in which Ben threw himself back in his chair, and the condescending manner in which he assured the waiter that the steak was "a prime article," could hardly have been surpassed in the most aristocratic circles.

"Well, Mark, have you had enough?" asked Ben.

"Yes," said Mark.

"Well, I haven't," said Ben. "I guess I'll have some puddin'. Look here, Johnny," to the colored waiter, "just bring a feller a plate of apple dump with both kinds of sauce."

After giving this liberal order Ben tilted his chair back, and began to pick his teeth with his fork. He devoted himself with assiduity to the consumption of the pudding, and concluded his expensive repast by the purchase of a two-cent cigar, with which he ascended to the street.

"Better have a cigar, Mark," he said.

"No, thank you," said the match boy. "I think I'd rather not."

'Oh, you're feared of being sick. You'll come to it in time. All business men smoke."

It is unnecessary to dwell upon the events of the afternoon. Mark was satisfied with the result of his morning's work, and waited about with Ben till the close of the afternoon, when the question came up, as to where the night should be passed.

"I guess we'd better go to the Lodge," said Ben 'Were you ever there?"

"No," said Mark.

"Well, come along. They'll give us a jolly bed, all for six cents, and there's a good, warm room to stay in. Then we can get breakfast in the mornin for six cents more."

"All right," said Mark. "We'll go."

The down-town Newsboys' Lodging House was at that time located at the corner of Fulton and Nassau Streets. It occupied the fifth and sixth stories of the building then known as the "Sun" building, owned by Moses S. Beach, the publisher of that journal. In the year 1868 circumstances rendered it expedi-dient to remove the Lodge to a building in Park Place. It is to be hoped that at some day not far distant the Children's Aid Society. who carry on this beneficent institution, will be able to erect a building of their own in some eligible locality, which can be permanently devoted to a purpose so praiseworthy.

Ben and Mark soon reached the entrance to the Lodge on Fulton Street. They ascended several flights of narrow stairs till they reached the top story. Then, opening a door at the left, they found themselves in the main room of the Lodge. It was a low-studded room of considerable dimensions, amply supplied with windows, looking out on Fulton and Nassau Streets. At the side nearest the door was a low platform, separated from the rest of the room by a railing. On this platform were a table and two or three chairs. This was the place for the superintendent, and for gentlemen who from time to time address the boys.

The superintendent at that time was Mr. Charles O'Connor, who still retains the office. Probably no one could be found better adapted to the difficult task of managing the class of boys who avail themselves of the good offices of the Newsboys' Home. His mild yet firm manner, and more than all the conviction that he is their friend, and feels a hearty interest in their welfare, secure a degree of decorum and good behavior which could hardly be anticipated. Oaths and vulgar speech, however common in the street, are rarely heard here, or, if heard, meet with instant rebuke.

The superintendent was in the room when Ben and Mark entered.

"Well, Ben, what luck have you had to-day?" said Mr. O'Connor.

"Pretty good," said Ben.

"And who is that with you?"

"Mother Watson's nephew," said Ben, with a grimace.

"He's only joking, sir," said Mark. "My name is Mark Manton."

"I am glad to see you, Mark," said the superintendent. "What is your business?"

"I sell matches, sir."

"Have you parents living?"

"No, sir; they are both dead."

"Where have you been living?"

"In Vandewater Street."

"With any one?"

"Yes, with a woman they call Mother Watson."

"Is she a relation of yours?"

"No, sir," said Mark, hastily.

"What sort of a woman is she?"

"Bad enough, sir. She gets drunk about every day, and used to beat me with a strap when I did not bring home as much money as she expected."

"So you have left her?"

"Yes, sir."

"Have you ever been up here before?"

"No, sir."

"I suppose you know the rules of the place."

"Yes, sir; Ben has told me."

"You had better go and wash. We shall have supper pretty quick. Have you any money?"

"Yes, sir."

Mark took out his hoard of money, and showed it to the superintendent, who was surprised at the amount.

"How did you get so much?" he asked.

"Part of it was given me," said Mark.

"What are you going to do with it? You don't need it all?"

"Will you keep it for me, sir?"

"I will put as much of it as you can spare into the bank for you. This is our bank."

He pointed to a table beside the railing on the outside. The top of it was pierced with narrow slits, each having a number attached. Each compartment was assigned to any boy who desired it, and his daily earnings were dropped in at the end of the day. Once a month the bank was opened, and the depositor was at liberty to withdraw his savings if he desired it. This is an excellent arrangement, as it has a tendency to teach frugal habits to the young patrons of the Lodge. Extravagance is one of their besetting sins. Many average a dollar and over as daily earnings, yet are always ragged and out at elbows, and often are unsupplied with the small price of a night's lodging at the Home. The money is squandered on gambling, cigars, and theatre-going, while the same sum would make them comfortable and independent of charity. The disposition to save is generally the first encouraging symptom in a street boy, and shows that he has really a desire to rise above his circumstances, and gain a respectable position in the world.

Ben, who had long frequented the Lodging House off and on, led the way to the washing-room, where Mark, to his satisfaction, was able to cleanse himself from the dust and impurity of the street. At Mother Watson's he had had no accommodations of the kind, as the old lady was not partial to water either internally or externally. He was forced to snatch such opportunities as he could find.

"Now," said Ben, "we'll go into the gymnasium."

A room opposite the main room had been fitted up with a few of the principal appliances of a gymnasium, and these were already in use by quite a number of boys.

Mark looked on, but did not participate, partly from bashfulness, and partly because he did not very well understand the use of the different appliances.

"How do you like it?" asked Ben.

"Very much," said Mark, with satisfaction. "I'm glad you brought me here."

"I'll show you the beds by and by," said Ben.

The rooms on the floor below were used for lodging. Tiers of neat beds, some like those in a steamboat or a hospital, filled a large room. They were very neat in appearance, and looked comfortable. In order to insure their continuing neat, the superintendent requires such as need it to wash their feet before retiring to bed

The supper was of course plain, but of good quality and sufficient quantity.

About nine o'clock Mark got into the neat bed which was assigned him, and felt that it was more satisfactory even than the cabin of a Brooklyn ferry-boat. He slept peacefully except towards morning, when he dreamed that his old persecutor, Mother Watson, was about to apply the dreaded strap. He woke up terrified, but soon realized with deep satistion that he was no longer in her clutches.

CHAPTER XIII.

WHAT BEFELL THE MATCH BOY.

DURING the next three months Mark made his home at the Lodging House. He was easily able to meet the small charges of the Lodge for bed and breakfast, and saved up ten dollars besides in the bank. Ben Gibson began to look upon him as quite a capitalist.

"I don't see how you save up so much money, Mark," he said. "You don't earn more'n half as much as I do."

"It's because you spend so much, Ben. It costs you considerable for cigars and such things, you know, and then you go to the Old Bowery pretty often."

"A feller must have some fun," said Ben. "They've got a tearin' old play at the Bowery now You'd better come to-night."

Mark shook his head.

"I feel pretty tired when it comes night," he said. "I'd rather stay at home."

"You aint so tough as I am," said Ben.

"No," said Mark, "I don't feel very strong. I think something's the matter with me."

"Nothin' aint ever the matter with me," said Ben, complacently; "but you're a puny little chap, that look as if you might blow away some day."

It was now April, and the weather was of that mild character that saps the strength and produces a feeling of weakness and debility. Mark had been exposed during the winter to the severity of stormy weather, and more than once got thoroughly drenched. It was an exposure that Ben would only have laughed at, but Mark was slightly built, without much strength of constitution, and he had been feeling very languid for a few days, so that it was with an effort that he dragged himself round during the day with his little bundle of matches.

This conversation with Ben took place in the morning just as both boys were going to work.

They separated at the City Hall Park, Ben finding a customer in front of the "Times" building, while Mark, after a little deliberation, decided to go on to

Pearl Street with his matches. He had visited the offices in most of the lower streets, but this was a new region to him, and he thought he might meet with better success there. So he kept on his way.

The warm sun and the sluggish air made his head ache, and he felt little disposition to offer his wares for sale. He called at one or two offices, but effected no sales. At length he reached a large warehouse with these names displayed on the sign over the door · —

"ROCKWELL & COOPER."

This, as the reader will remember, was the establishment in which Richard Hunter, formerly Ragged Dick, was now book-keeper.

At this point a sudden faintness came over Mark, and he sank to the ground insensible.

A moment before Richard Hunter handed a couple of letters to the office boy, — known to the readers of the earlier volumes in this series as Micky Maguire, — and said, "Michael, I should like to have you carry these at once to the post-office. On the way you may stop at Trescott & Wayne's, and get this bill cashed, if possible."

"All right, Mr. Hunter," said Michael, respectfully.

Richard Hunter and Micky Maguire had been boot-blacks together, and had had more than one contest for the supremacy. They had been sworn enemies, and Micky had done his utmost to injure Richard, but the latter, by his magnanimity, had finally wholly overcome the antipathy of his former foe, and, when opportunity offered, had lifted him to a position in the office where he was himself employed. In return, Micky had become an enthusiastic admirer of Richard, and, so far from taking advantage of their former relations, had voluntarily taken up the habit of addressing him as Mr. Hunter.

Michael went out on his errand, but just outside the door came near stepping upon the prostrate form of the little match boy.

"Get up here!" he said, roughly, supposing at first that Mark had thrown himself down out of laziness and gone to sleep.

Mark didn't answer, and Micky, bending over, saw his fixed expression and waxen pallor.

"Maybe the little chap's dead," he thought, startled, and, without more ado, took him up in his strong arms and carried him into the counting-room.

"Wh: have you got there, Michael?" asked Richard Hunter, turning round in surprise.

"A little match boy that was lyin' just outside the door. He looks as if he might be dead."

Richard jumped at once from his stool, and, approaching the boy, looked earnestly in his face.

"He has fainted away," he said, after a pause. "Bring some water, quick!"

Micky brought a glass of water, which was thrown in the face of Mark. The match boy gave a little shiver, and, opening his eyes, fixed them upon Richard Hunter.

"Where am I?" he asked, vacantly

"You are with friends," said Richard, gently. "You were found at our door faint. Do you feel sick?"

"I feel weak," said Mark.

"Have you been well lately?"

"No, I've felt tired and weak."

"Are you a match boy?"

"Yes."

"Have you parents living?"

"No," said Mark.

"Poor fellow!" said Richard. "I know how to pity you. I have no parents either."

"But you have got money," said Mark. "You don't have to live in the street."

"I was once a street boy like you."

"You!" repeated the match boy, in surprise.

"Yes. But where do you sleep?"

"At the Lodging House."

"It is a good place. Michael, you had better go to the post-office now."

Mark looked about him a little anxiously.

"Where are my matches?" he asked.

"Just outside; I'll get them," said Michael, promptly.

He brought them in, and then departed on his errand.

"I guess I'd better be going," said Mark, rising feebly

"No," said Richard. "You are not able. Come here and sit down. You will feel stronger by and by. Did you eat any breakfast this morning?"

"A little," said Mark, "but I was not very hungry."

"Do you think you could eat anything now?"

Mark shook his head.

"No," he said, "I don't feel hungry. I only feel tired."

"Would you like to rest?"

"Yes. That's all I want."

"Come here then, and I will see what I can do for you."

Mark followed his new friend into the warehouse. where Richard found a soft bale of cotton, and told Mark he might lie down upon it. This the poor boy was glad enough to do. In his weakness he was disposed to sleep, and soon closed his eyes in slumber. Several times Richard went out to look at him, but found him dozing, and was unwilling to interrupt him.

The day wore away, and afternoon came.

Mark got up from his cotton bale, and with unsteady steps came to the door of the counting-room.

"I'm going," he said.

Richard turned round.

"Where are you going?"

"I'm going to the Lodge. I think I won't sell any more matches to-day."

"I'll take all you've left," said Richard. "Don't trouble yourself about them. But you are not going to the Lodge."

Mark looked at him in surprise.

"I shall take you home with me to-night," he said. "You are not well, and I will look after you. At the Lodge there will be a crowd of boys, and the noise will do you harm."

"You are very kind," said Mark; "but I'm afraid I'll trouble you."

"No," said Richard, "I shan't count it a trouble. I was once a poor boy like you, and I found friends. I'll be your friend. Go back and lie down again, and in about an hour I shall be ready to take you with me."

It seemed strange to Mark to think that there was somebody who proposed to protect and look after him. In many of the offices which he visited he met with rough treatment, and was ordered out of the way, as if he were a dog, and without human feelings. Many who treated him in this way were really kind-hearted men who had at home children whom they loved, but they appeared to forget that these neglected children of the street had feelings and wants as well as their own, who were tenderly nurtured. They did not remember that they were somebody's children, and that cold, and harshness, and want were as hard for them to bear as for those in a higher rank of life. But Mark was in that state of weakness when it seemed sweet to throw off all care or thought for the future, and to sink back upon the soft bale with the thought that he had nothing to do but to rest.

"That boy is going to be sick," thought Richard Hunter to himself. "I think he is going to have a fever."

It was because of this thought that he decided to carry him home. He had a kind heart, and he knew how terrible a thing sickness is to these little street waifs, who have no mother or sister to smooth their pillows, or cheer them with gentle words. The friendless condition of the little match boy touched his heart, and he resolved that, as he had the means of taking care of him, he would do so

"Michael," he said, at the close of business hours "I wish you would call a hack."

"What, to come here?" asked Micky, surprised.

"Yes. I am going to take that little boy home with me. I think he is going to be sick, and I am afraid he would have a hard time of it if I sent him back into the street."

"Bully for you, Mr. Hunter!" said Micky, who, though rough in his outward manners, was yet capable of appreciating kindness in others. There were times indeed in the past when he had treated smaller boys brutally, but it was under the influence of passion. He had improved greatly since, and his better nature was beginning to show itself.

Micky went out, and soon returned in state inside a hack. He was leaning back, thinking it would be a very good thing if he had a carriage of his own to ride in. But I am afraid that day will never come. Micky has already turned out much better than was expected, but he is hardly likely to rise much higher than the subordinate position he now occupies. In capacity and education he is far inferior to his old associate, Richard Hunter, who is destined to rise much higher than at present.

Richard Hunter went to the rear of the warehouse where Mark still lay on his bale.

"Come," he said; "we'll go home now."

Mark rose from his recumbent position, and walked to the door. He saw with surprise the carriage, the door of which Micky Maguire held open.

"Are we going to ride in that?" he asked.

"Yes," said Richard Hunter. "Let me help you in."

The little match boy sank back in the soft seat in vague surprise at his good luck. He could not help wondering what Ben Gibson would say if he could see him now.

Richard Hunter sat beside him, and supported Mark's head. The driver whipped up his horse, and they were speedily on their way up the Bowery to St. Mark's Place.

CHAPTER XIV.

RICHARD HUNTER'S WARD.

It was about half-past five o'clock in the afternoon when the carriage containing Richard Hunter and the match boy stopped in front of his boarding-place in St. Mark's Place. Richard helped the little boy out, saying, cheerfully, "Well, we've got home."

"Is this where you live?" asked Mark, faintly.

"Yes. How do you like it?"

"It's a nice place. I am afraid you are taking too much trouble about me."

"Don't think of that. Come in."

Richard had ascended the front steps, after paying the hackman, and taking out his night-key opened the outside door.

"Come upstairs," he said.

They ascended two flights of stairs, and Richard threw open the door of his room. A fire was already burning in the grate, and it looked bright and cheerful.

"Do you feel tired?" asked Richard.

"Yes, a little."

"Then lie right down on the bed. You are hungry too, — are you not?"

"A little."

"I will have something sent up to you."

Just then Fosdick, who, it will be remembered, was Richard Hunter's room-mate, entered the room. He looked with surprise at Mark, and then inquiringly at Richard.

"It is a little match boy," explained the latter, "who fell in a fainting-fit in front of our office. I think the poor fellow is going to be sick, so I brought him home, and mean to take care of him till he is well."

"You must let me share the expense, Dick," said Fosdick.

"No, but I'll let you share the care of him. That will do just as well."

"But I would rather share the expense. He reminds me of the way I was situated when I fell in with you. What is your name?"

"Mark Manton," said the match boy.

"I've certainly seen him somewhere before," said Fosdick, reflectively. "His face looks familiar to me."

"So it does to me. Perhaps I've seen him about the streets somewhere."

"I have it," said Fosdick, suddenly; "don't you remember the boy we saw sleeping in the cabin of the Fulton Ferryboat?"

"Yes."

"I think he is the one. Mark," he continued turning to the match boy, "didn't you sleep one night on a Brooklyn ferry-boat about three months ago?"

"Yes," said Mark.

"And did you find anything in your vest-pocket in the morning?"

"Yes," said the match boy with interest. "I found a dollar, and didn't know where it came from. Was it you that put it in?"

"He had a hand in it," said Fosdick, pointing with a smile to his room-mate.

"I was very glad to get it," said Mark. "I only had eight cents besides, and that gave me

10

enough to buy some matches. That was at the time I ran away."

"Who did you run away from?"

"From Mother Watson."

"Mother Watson?" repeated Dick. "I wonder if I don't know her. She is a very handsome old lady, with a fine red complexion, particularly about the nose."

"Yes," said Mark with a smile.

"And she takes whiskey when she can get it?"

"Yes."

"How did you fall in with her?"

"She promised to take care of me when my mother died, but instead of that she wanted me to earn money for her."

"Yes, she was always a very disinterested old lady. So it appears you didn't like her as a guardian?"

"No."

"Then suppose you take me. Would you like to be my ward?"

"I think I would, but I don't know what it means," said Mark.

"It means that I'm to look after you," said Dick,

"just as if I was your uncle or grandfather. You may call me grandfather if you want to."

"Oh, you're too young," said Mark, amused in spite of his weakness.

"Then we won't decide just at present about the name. But I forgot all about your being hungry."

"I'm not very hungry."

"At any rate you haven't had anything to eat since morning, and need something. I'll go down and see Mrs. Wilson about it."

Richard Hunter soon explained matters to Mrs. Wilson, to whom he offered to pay an extra weekly sum for Mark, and arranged that a small single bed should be placed in one corner of the room temporarily in which the match boy should sleep. He speedily reappeared with a bowl of broth, a cup of tea, and some dry toast. The sight of these caused the match boy's eyes to brighten, and he was able to do very good justice to all.

"Now," said Richard Hunter, "I will call in a doctor, and find out what is the matter with my little ward."

In the course of the evening Dr. Pemberton, a young dispensary physician, whose acquaintance

Richard had casually made, called at his request and looked at the patient.

"He is not seriously sick," he pronounced. "It is chiefly debility that troubles him, brought on probably by exposure, and over-exertion in this languid spring weather."

"Then you don't think he is going to have a fever?" said Dick.

"No, not if he remains under your care. Had he continued in the street, I think he would not have escaped one."

"What shall we do for him?"

"Rest is most important of all. That, with nourishing food and freedom from exposure, will soon bring him round again."

"He shall have all these."

"I suppose you know him, as you take so much interest in him?"

"No, I never saw him but once before to-day, but I am able to befriend him, and he has no other friends."

"There are not many young men who would take all this trouble about a poor match boy," said the doctor.

"It's because they don't know how hard it is to be friendless and neglected," said Dick. "I've known that feeling, and it makes me pity those who are in the same condition I once was."

"I wish there were more like you, Mr. Hunter," said Dr. Pemberton. "There would be less suffering in the world. As to our little patient here, I have no doubt he will do well, and soon be on his legs again."

Indeed Mark was already looking better and feeling better. The rest which he had obtained during the day, and the refreshment he had just taken, were precisely what he needed. He soon fell asleep, and Richard and Fosdick, lighting the gas lamp on the centre-table, sat down to their evening studies.

In a few days Mark was decidedly better, but it was thought best that he should still keep the room. He liked it very well in the evening when Dick and Fosdick were at home, but he felt rather lonesome in the daytime. Richard Hunter thought of this one day, and said, "Can you read, Mark?"

"Yes," said the match boy.

"Who taught you? Not Mother Watson, surely."

"No, she couldn't read herself. It was my mother who taught me."

"I think I must get you two or three books of stories to read while we are away in the day-time."

"You are spending too much money for me, Mr Hunter."

"Remember I am your guardian, and it is my duty to take care of you."

The next morning on his way down town, Richard Hunter stepped into a retail bookstore on Broadway. As he entered, a boy, if indeed it be allowable to apply such a term to a personage so consequential in his manners, came forward.

"What, Roswell Crawford, are you here?" asked Richard Hunter, in surprise.

Roswell, who has already been mentioned in this story, and who figured considerably in previous volumes of this series, answered rather stiffly to this salutation.

"Yes," he said. "I am here for a short time. I came in to oblige Mr. Baker."

"You were always very obliging, Roswell," said Richard, good-humoredly.

Roswell did not appear to appreciate this compliment. He probably thought it savored of irony.

"Do you want to buy anything this morning?" he said, shortly

"Yes; I would like to look at some books of fairy stories."

"For your own reading, I suppose," said Roswell.

"I may read them, but I am getting them for my ward."

"Is he a boot-black?" sneered Roswell, who knew all about Dick's early career.

"No," said Richard, "he's a match boy; so if you've got any books that you can warrant to be just the thing for match boys, I should like to see them."

"We don't have many customers of that class," said Roswell, unpleasantly. "They generally go to cheaper establishments, when they are able to read."

"Do they?" said Dick. "I'm glad you've got into a place where you only meet the cream of society," and Dick glanced significantly at a red-nosed man who came in to buy a couple of sheets of note-paper.

Roswell colored.

"There are some exceptions," he said, and glanced pointedly at Richard Hunter himself.

"Well," said Dick, after looking over a collection of juvenile books, "I'll take these two."

He drew out his pocket-book, and handed Roswell a ten-dollar bill. Roswell changed it with a feeling of jealousy and envy. He was the "son of a gentleman," as he often boasted, but he never had a ten-dollar bill in his pocket. Indeed, he was now working for six dollars a week, and glad to get that, after having been out of a situation for several months.

Just then Mr. Gladden, of the large down-town firm of Gladden & Co., came into the store, and, seeing Richard, saluted him cordially.

"How are you this morning, Mr. Hunter?" he said. "Are you on your way down town?"

"Yes, sir," said Richard.

"Come with me. We will take an omnibus together;" and the two walked out of the store in familiar conversation.

"I shouldn't think such a man as Mr. Gladden would notice a low boot-black," said Roswell, bitterly.

The rest of the day he was made unhappy by the thought of Dick's prosperity, and his own hard fate, in being merely a clerk in a bookstore with a salary of six dollars a week.

CHAPTER XV.

MARK GETS A PLACE.

IN a week from the purchase of the books, Mark felt that he was fully recovered. He never had much color, but the unhealthy pallor had left his cheeks, and he had an excellent appetite.

"Well, Mark, how do you feel to-night?" asked Richard, on his return from the store one evening.

"I'm all right, now, Mr. Hunter. I think I will go to work to-morrow morning."

"What sort of work?"

"Selling matches."

"Do you like to sell matches?"

"I like it better than selling papers, or blacking boots."

"But wouldn't you like better to be in a store?"

"I couldn't get a place," said Mark.

"Why not?"

"My clothes are ragged," said the match boy with

some hesitation. "Besides I haven't got anybody to refer to."

"Can't you refer to your guardian?" asked Richard Hunter, smiling.

"Do you think I had better try to get a place in a store, Mr. Hunter?" asked Mark.

"Yes, I think it would be much better for you than to sell matches on the street. You are not a strong boy, and the exposure is not good for you. As to your clothes, we'll see if we cannot supply you with something better than you have on."

"But," said Mark, "I want to pay for my clothes myself. I have got ten dollars in the bank at the Newsboys' Lodge."

"Very well. You can go down to-morrow morning and get it. But we needn't wait for that. I will go and get you some clothes before I go to business."

In the morning Richard Hunter went out with the match boy, and for twenty dollars obtained for him a very neat gray suit, besides a supply of under-clothing. Mark put them on at once, and felt not a little pleased with the improvement in his appearance.

"You can carry your old clothes to Mr. O'Connor," said Richard. "They are not very good, but they are better than none, and he may have an opportunity of giving them away."

"You have been very kind to me, Mr. Hunter," said Mark, gratefully. "Good-by."

"Good-by? What makes you say that?"

"Because I am going now to the Newsboys' Lodge."

"Yes, but you are coming back again."

"But I think I had better go there to live now. It will be much cheaper, and I ought not to put you to so much expense."

"You're a good boy, Mark, but you must remember that I am your guardian, and am to be obeyed as such. You're not going back to the Lodge to live. I have arranged to have you stay with me at my boarding-place. As soon as you have got a place you will work in the daytime, and every Saturday night you will bring me your money. In the evening I shall have you study a little, for I don't want you to grow up as ignorant as I was at your age."

"Were you ignorant, Mr. Hunter?" asked Mark, with interest

"Yes, I was," said Richard. "When I was fourteen, I couldn't read nor write."

"I can hardly believe that, Mr. Hunter," said Mark. "You're such a fine scholar."

"Am I?" asked Richard, smiling, yet well pleased with the compliment.

"Why, you can read French as fast as I can read English, and write beautifully."

"Well, I had to work hard to do it," said Richard Hunter. "But I feel paid for all the time I've spent in trying to improve myself. Sometimes I've thought I should like to spend the evening at some place of amusement rather than in study; but if I had, there'd be nothing to show for it now. Take my advice, Mark, and study all you can, and you'll grow up respectable and respected."

"Now," he added, after a pause, "I'll tell you what you may do. You may look in my 'Herald' every morning, and whenever you see a boy advertised for you can call, or whenever, in going along the street, you see a notice 'Boy wanted,' you may call in, and sooner or later you'll get something. If they ask for references, you may refer to Richard Hunter book-keeper for Rockwell & Cooper."

"Thank you, Mr. Hunter," said Mark. "I will do so."

On parting with his guardian the match boy went down town to the Lodging House. The superintendent received him kindly.

"I didn't know what had become of you, Mark," he said. "If it had been some of the boys, I should have been afraid they had got into a scrape, and gone to the Island. But I didn't think that of you."

"I hope you'll never hear that of me, Mr. O'Connor," said Mark.

"I hope not. I'm always sorry to hear of any boy's going astray. But you seem to have been doing well since I saw you;" and the superintendent glanced at Mark's new clothes.

"I've met with some kind friends," said the match boy. "I have been sick, and they took care of me."

"And now you have come back to the Lodge."

"Yes, but not to stay. I came for the money that I have saved up in the bank. It is going for these clothes."

"Very well. You shall have it. What is the name of the friend who has taken care of you?"

"Richard Hunter."

"I know him," said the superintendent. "He is an excellent young man. You could not be in better hands."

On leaving the Lodge Mark felt a desire to find his old ally, Ben Gibson, who, though rather a rough character, had been kind to him.

Ben was not difficult to find. During business hours he was generally posted on Nassau Street, somewhere between Fulton Street and Spruce Street.

He was just polishing off a customer's boots when Mark came up, and touched him lightly on the shoulder. Ben looked up, but did not at first recognize the match boy in the neatly dressed figure before him.

"Shine yer boots!" he asked, in a professional tone.

"Why, Ben, don't you know me?" asked Mark, laughing.

"My eyes, if it aint Mark, the match boy!" exclaimed Ben, in surprise. "Where've you been all this while, Mark?"

"I've been sick, Ben."

"I'd like to be sick too, if that's the way you got them clo'es. I didn't know what had 'come of you.'

"I found some good friends," said Mark.

"If your friends have got any more good clo'es they want to get rid of," said Ben, "tell 'em you know a chap that can take care of a few. Are you in the match business now?"

"I haven't been doing anything for three weeks," said Mark.

"Goin' to sell matches again?"

"No."

"Sellin' papers?"

"No, I'm trying to find a place in a store."

"I don't think I'd like to be in a store," said Ben, reflectively. "I'm afraid my delicate constitution couldn't stand the confinement. Besides, I'm my own boss now, and don't have nobody to order me round."

"But you don't expect to black boots all your life, Ben, do you?"

"I dunno," said Ben. "Maybe when I'm married, I'll choose some other business. It would be rather hard to support a family at five cents a shine. Are you comin' to the Lodge to-night?"

"No," said Mark, "I'm boarding up at St. Mark's Place."

"Mother Watson hasn't opened a fashionable boardin'-house up there, has she?"

"I guess not," said Mark, smiling. "I can't think what has become of her. I haven't seen her since the day she tried to carry me off."

"I've heard of her," said Ben. "She's stoppin' with some friends at the Island. They won't let her come away on account of likin' her company so much."

"I hope I shall never see her again," said Mark, with a shudder. "She is a wicked old woman. But I must be going, Ben."

"I s'pose you'll come and see a feller now and then."

"Yes, Ben, when I get time. But I hope to get a place soon."

Mark walked leisurely up Broadway. Having been confined to the house for three weeks, he enjoyed the excitement of being out in the street once more. The shop windows looked brighter and gayer than before, and the little match boy felt that the world was a very pleasant place after all.

He had passed Eighth Street before he was fairly aware of the distance he had traversed. He found himself looking into the window of a bookstore. While examining the articles in the window his eye suddenly caught the notice pasted in the middle of the glass on a piece of white paper: —

"BOY WANTED."

"Perhaps they'll take me," thought Mark, suddenly. "At any rate I'll go in and see."

Accordingly he entered the store, and looked about him a little undecidedly.

"Well, sonny, what do you want?" asked a clerk.

"I see that you want a boy," said Mark.

"Yes. Do you want a place?"

"I am trying to get one."

"Well, go and see that gentleman about it."

He pointed to a gentleman who was seated at a desk in the corner of the store.

"Please, sir, do you want a boy?" he asked.

"Yes," said the gentleman. "How old are you?"

"Ten years old."

"You are rather young. Have you been in any place before?"

"No, sir."

"Do you know your way about the city pretty well?"

"Yes, sir."

"I want a boy to deliver papers and magazines, and carry small parcels of books. Do you think you could do that?"

"Yes, sir."

"Without stopping to play on the way?"

"Yes, sir."

"I have just discharged one boy, because he was gone an hour and a half on an errand to Twentieth Street. You are the first boy that has answered my advertisement. I'll try you on a salary of three dollars a week, if you can go to work at once. What is your name?"

"Mark Manton."

"Very well, Mark. Go to Mr. Jones, behind the counter there, and he will give you a parcel to carry to West Twenty-First Street."

"I'm in luck," thought Mark. "I didn't expect to get a place so easily."

CHAPTER XVI.

MARK'S FIRST IMPRESSIONS.

PROBABLY my readers already understand that the bookstore in which Mark has secured a place is the same in which Roswell Crawford is employed. This circumstance, if Mark had only known it, was likely to make his position considerably less desirable than it would otherwise have been. Mr. Baker, the proprietor of the store, was very considerate in his treatment of those in his employ, and Mr. Jones, his chief clerk, was good-natured and pleasant. But Roswell was very apt to be insolent and disagreeable to those who were, or whom he considered to be, in an inferior position to himself, while his lofty ideas of his own dignity and social position as the "son of a gentleman," made him not very desirable as a clerk. Still he had learned something from his bad luck thus far. He had been so long in getting his present place, that he felt it prudent to sacrifice his pride to some extent for the sake of retaining it. But if he could neglect his duties without attracting attention, he resolved to do it, feeling that six dollars was a beggarly salary for a young gentleman of his position and capacity. It was unfortunate for him, and a source of considerable annoyance, that he could get no one except his mother to assent to his own estimate of his abilities. Even his Cousin Gilbert, who had been Rockwell & Cooper's bookkeeper before Richard Hunter succeeded to the position, did not conceal his poor opinion of Roswell; but this the latter attributed to prejudice, being persuaded in his own mind that his cousin was somewhat inclined to be envious of his superior abilities.

At the time that Mark was so suddenly engaged by Mr. Baker, Roswell had gone out to dinner. When he returned, Mark had gone out with the parcel to West Twenty-first Street. So they missed each other just at first.

"Well, Crawford," said Mr. Jones, as Roswell re-entered the store, "Mr. Baker has engaged a new boy."

"Has he? What sort of a fellow is he?"

"A little fellow. He doesn't look as if he was more than ten years old."

"Where is he?"

"Mr. Baker sent him on an errand to Twenty-first Street."

"Humph!" said Roswell, a little discontented, "I was going to recommend a friend of mine."

"There may be a chance yet. This boy may not suit."

In about five minutes Mr. Baker and Mr. Jones both went out to dinner. It was the middle of the day, when there is very little business, and it would not be difficult for Roswell to attend to any customers who might call.

As soon as he was left alone, Roswell got an interesting book from the shelves, and, sitting down in his employer's chair, began to read, though this was against the rules in business hours. To see the pompous air with which Roswell threw himself back in his chair, it might have been supposed that he was the proprietor of the establishment, though I believe it is true, as a general rule, that employers are not in the habit of putting on so many airs, unless the position is a new one, and they have not yet got over the new feeling of importance which it is apt to inspire at first.

While Roswell was thus engaged Mark returned from his errand.

He looked about him in some uncertainty on entering the store, not seeing either Mr. Baker or the chief clerk.

"Come here," said Roswell, in a tone of authority.

Mark walked up to the desk.

"So you are the new boy?" said Roswell, after a close scrutiny.

"Yes."

"It would be a little more polite to say 'Yes sir.'"

"Yes, sir."

"What is your age?"

"Ten years."

"Humph! You are rather young. If I had been consulted I should have said 'Get a boy of twelve years old.'"

"I hope I shall suit," said Mark.

"I hope so," said Roswell, patronizingly. "You will find us very easy to get along with if you do your duty. We were obliged to send away a boy this morning because he played instead of going on his errands at once"

Mark could not help wondering what was Roswell's position in the establishment. He talked as if he were one of the proprietors; but his youthful appearance made it difficult to suppose that.

"What is your name?" continued Roswell.

"Mark Manton."

"Have you been in any place before?"

"No, sir."

"Do you live with your parents?"

"My parents are dead."

"Then whom do you live with?"

"With my guardian."

"So you have a guardian?" said Roswell, a little surprised. "What is his name?"

"Mr. Hunter."

"Hunter!" repeated Roswell, hastily. "What is his first name?"

"Richard I believe."

"Dick Hunter!" exclaimed Roswell, scornfully "Do you mean to say that he has charge of you?"

"Yes," said Mark, firmly, for he perceived the tone in which his friend was referred to, and resented it. Moreover the new expression which came over Roswell's face brought back to his recollection the evening when, for the first time in his life, he had begged in Fulton Market, and been scornfully repulsed by Roswell and his mother. Roswell's face had at first seemed familiar to him, but it was only now that he recognized him. Roswell, on the other hand, was not likely to identify the neatly dressed boy before him with the shivering little beggar of the market. But it recurred to him all at once that Dick had referred to his ward as a match boy.

"You were a match boy?" he said, in the manner of one making a grave accusation.

"Yes, sir."

"Then why didn't you keep on selling matches, and not try to get a place in a respectable store?"

"Because Mr. Hunter thought it better for me to go into a store."

"Mr. Hunter! Perhaps you don't know that your guardian, as you call him, used to be a boot-black."

"Yes, he told me so."

"They called him 'Ragged Dick' then," said Roswell, turning up his nose. "He couldn't read or write, I believe."

"He's a good scholar now," said Mark.

"Humph! I suppose he told you so. But you mustn't believe all he tells you."

"He wouldn't tell anything but the truth," said Mark, who was bolder in behalf of his friend than he would have been for himself.

"So he did tell you he was a good scholar? I thought so."

"No, he told me nothing about it; but since I have lived with him I've heard him read French as well as English."

"Perhaps that isn't saying much," said Roswell, with a sneer. "Can you read yourself?"

"Yes."

"That is more than I expected. What induced Mr. Baker to take a boy from the street is more than I can tell."

"I suppose I can run errands just as well, if I was once a match boy," said Mark, who did not fancy the tone which Roswell assumed towards him, and began to doubt whether he was a person of as much importance as he at first supposed.

"We shall see," said Roswell, loftily. "But there's one thing I'll advise you, young man, and that is, to treat me with proper respect. You'll find it best to keep friends with me. I can get you turned away any time."

Mark hardly knew whether to believe this or not. He already began to suspect that Roswell was something of a humbug, and though it was not in his nature to form a causeless dislike, he certainly did not feel disposed to like Roswell. He did not care so much for any slighting remarks upon himself, as for the scorn with which Roswell saw fit to speak of his friend, Richard Hunter, who by his good offices had won the little boy's lasting gratitude. Mark did not reply to the threat contained in these last words of Roswell.

"Is there anything for me to do?" he asked.

"Yes, you may dust off those books on the counter. There's the duster hanging up."

This was really Roswell's business, and he ought to have been at work in this way instead of reading; but it was characteristic of him to shift his duties upon others. He was not aware of how much time had passed, and supposed that Mark would be through before Mr. Barker returned. But that gentleman came in while Roswell was busily engaged in reading.

"Is that the way you do your work, Roswell?" asked his employer.

Roswell jumped to his feet in some confusion.

"I thought I had better set the new boy to work," he said.

"Dusting the books is your work, not his."

"He was doing nothing, sir."

"He will have plenty to do in carrying out parcels. Besides, I don't know that it is any worse for him to be idle than you. You were reading also, which you know is against the rules of the store."

Roswell made no reply, but it hurt his pride considerably to be censured thus in presence of Mark, to whom he had spoken with such an assumption of power and patronage.

"I wish I had a store of my own," he thought, discontentedly. "Then I could do as I pleased without having anybody to interfere with me."

But Roswell did not understand, and there are

plenty of boys in the same state of ignorance, that those who fill subordinate positions acceptably are most likely to rise to stations where they will themselves have control over others.

"I suppose you have not been to dinner," said Mr. Baker, turning to Mark.

"No, sir."

"You board in St. Mark's Place, I think you said?"

"Yes, sir."

"Very well, here is a parcel to go to East Ninth Street. You may call and leave that at the address marked upon it, and may stay out long enough for dinner. But don't be gone more than an hour in all."

"No, sir."

"I am glad that boy isn't my employer," thought Mark, referring of course to Roswell Crawford, who, by the way, would have been indignant at such an appellation. "I like Mr. Baker a great deal better."

Mark was punctual to his appointment, and in a little less than an hour reported himself at the store again for duty.

CHAPTER XVII.

BAD ADVICE.

ROSWELL pursued his way home with a general sense of discontent. Why should he be so much worse off than Richard Hunter, who had only been a ragged boot-black three years before? The whole world seemed to be in a conspiracy to advance Richard, and to keep him down. To think he should be only earning six dollars a week, while Dick, whom he considered so far beneath him, was receiving twenty, was really outrageous. And now he had pushed a low dependent of his into Baker's store where Roswell was obliged to associate with him!

Certainly Roswell's grievances were numerous. But there was one thing he did not understand, that the greatest obstacle to his advancement was himself. If he had entered any situation with the determination to make his services valuable, and discharge his duties, whatever they might be, with conscientious fidelity, he would have found his relations with his employer much more agreeable and satisfactory.

Mrs. Crawford still kept the house in Clinton Place, letting nearly all the rooms to lodgers. In this way she succeeded in making both ends meet though with considerable difficulty, so that she had not the means to supply Roswell with the spending money he desired. Her nephew, James Gilbert, Richard Huntley's predecessor as book-keeper, still boarded with her. It will be remembered by the readers of "Fame and Fortune," that this Gilbert, on being questioned by Mr. Rockwell as to his share in the plot against Dick, had angrily resigned his position, thinking, probably, that he should lose it at any rate.

It so happened that business was generally depressed at this time, and it was three months before he succeeded in obtaining another place, and then he was compelled to work for eight hundred dollars, or two hundred less than he had formerly received. This was a great disappointment to him, and did not help his temper much, which had never been very sweet. He felt quite exasperated against Dick, whom, very much against his wishes, he had been the means of promoting to his own place. Indeed, on this point, he sympathized heartily with Roswell, whose dislike to Richard Hunter has already been shown.

"Well, mother," said Roswell, as he entered Mrs. Crawford's presence, "I'm getting tired of Baker's store."

"Don't say so, Roswell," said his mother, in alarm. "Remember how long it took you to get the place."

"I have to work like a dog for six dollars a week," said Roswell.

"Yes," said his cousin, with a sneer, "that's precisely the way you work. Dogs spend their time running round the street doing nothing."

"Well, I have to work hard enough," said Roswell, "but I wouldn't mind that so much, if I didn't have to associate with low match boys."

"What do you mean, Roswell?" asked his mother, who did not understand the allusion.

"Baker hired a new boy to-day, and who do you think he turns out to be?"

"Not that boy, Ragged Dick?"

"No, you don't think he would give up Cousin James' place, where he gets a thousand dollars a year, to go into Baker's as boy?"

"Who was it, then?"

"He used to be a ragged match boy about the streets Dick Hunter picked him up somewhere, and got him a situation in our store, on purpose to spite me, I expect."

As the reader is aware, Roswell was mistaken in his supposition, as Mark obtained the place on his own responsibility.

"The boot-black seems to be putting on airs," said Mrs. Crawford.

"Yes, he pretends to be the guardian of this match boy."

"What's the boy's name?"

"Mark Manton."

"If I were Mr. Baker," said Mrs. Crawford "I should be afraid to take a street boy into my employ. Very likely he isn't honest."

"I wish he would steal something," said Roswell, not very charitably. "Then we could get rid of him, and the boot-black would be pretty well mortified about it."

"He'll be found out sooner or later," said Mrs Crawford. "You may depend on that. You'd better keep a sharp lookout for him, Roswell. If you catch him in stealing, it will help you with Mr. Baker, or ought to."

This would have comforted Roswell more, but that he was privately of opinion that Mark was honest, and would not be likely to give him any chance of detecting him in stealing. Still, by a little manage ment on his part, he might cause him to fall under suspicion. It would of course be miserably mean on his part to implicate a little boy in a false charge; but Roswell *was* a mean boy, and he was not scrupulous where his dislike was concerned. He privately decided to think over this new plan for getting Mark into trouble.

"Isn't dinner ready, mother?" he asked, rather impatiently.

"It will be in about ten minutes."

"I'm as hungry as a bear."

"You can always do your part at the table," said his cousin unpleasantly.

"I don't know why I shouldn't. I have to work hard enough."

"You are always talking about your hard work. My belief is that you don't earn your wages."

"I should think it was a pity if I didn't earn six dollars a week," said Roswell.

"Come, James, you're always hard on Roswell," said Mrs. Crawford. "I am sure he has hard times enough without his own relations turning against him."

James Gilbert did not reply. He was naturally of a sarcastic turn, and, seeing Roswell's faults, was not inclined to spare them. He might have pointed them out, however, in a kindly manner, and then his young cousin might possibly been benefited; but Gilbert felt very little interest in Roswell.

Immediately after dinner Roswell took up his cap. His mother observed this, and inquired, "Where are you going, Roswell?"

"I'm going out to walk."

"Why don't you go with your cousin?'

James Gilbert had also taken his hat.

"He don't want to be bothered with me," said Roswell, and this statement Gilbert did not take the trouble to contradict.

"Why can't you stay in and read?"

"I haven't got anything to read. Besides I've been cooped up in the store all day, and I want to breathe a little fresh air."

There was reason in this, and his mother did not gainsay it, but still she felt that it was not quite safe for a boy to spend his evenings out in a large city, without any one to look after him.

Roswell crossed Broadway, and, proceeding down Eighth Street, met a boy of about his own age in front of the Cooper Institute.

"How long have you been waiting, Ralph?" he asked.

"Not long. I only just came up."

"I couldn't get away as soon as I expected. Dinner was rather late."

"Have a cigar, Roswell?" asked Ralph.

"Yes," said Roswell, "I don't mind."

"You'll find these cigars pretty good. I paid ten cents apiece."

"I don't see how you can afford it," said Roswell "Your cigars must cost you considerable."

"I don't always buy ten-centers. Generally I pay only five cents."

"Well, that mounts up when you smoke three or

four in a day. Let me see, what wages do you get?"

"Seven dollars a week."

"That's only a dollar more than I get," said Roswell.

"I know one thing, it's miserably small," said Ralph. "We ought to get twice what we do."

"These shop-keepers are awfully mean," said Roswell, beginning to puff away at his cigar

"That's so."

"But still you always seem to have plenty of money. That's what puzzles me," said Roswell. "I'm always pinched. I have to pay my mother all my wages but a dollar a week. And what's a dollar?" he repeated, scornfully.

"Well," said Ralph, "my board costs me all but a dollar. So we are about even there."

"Do you pay your board out of your earnings?"

"I have to. My governor won't foot the bills, so I have to."

"Still you seem to have plenty of money," persisted Roswell.

"Yes, I look out for that," said Ralph Graham, ignificantly.

"But I don't see how you manage. I might look out all day, and I wouldn't be any the better off."

"Perhaps you don't go the right way to work," said his companion, taking the cigar from his mouth, and knocking off the ashes.

"Then I wish you'd tell me the right way."

"Why, the fact is," said Ralph, slowly, "I make my employer pay me higher wages than he thinks he does."

"I don't see how you can do that," said Roswell, who didn't yet understand.

Ralph took the cigar, now nearly smoked out, from his mouth, and threw it on the pavement. He bent towards Roswell, and whispered something in his ear. Roswell started and turned pale.

"But," he said, "that's dishonest."

"Hush!" said Ralph, "don't speak so loud. Oughtn't employers to pay fair wages,—tell me that?"

"Certainly."

"But if they don't and won't, what then?"

"I don't know."

"Well, I do. We must help ourselves, that is all."

"But," said Roswell, "what would be thought of you if it were found out?"

"There's plenty of clerks that do it. Bless you, it's expected. I heard a man say once that he expected to lose about so much by his clerks."

"But I think it would be better to pay good wages."

"So do I, only you see they won't do it."

"How much do you — do you make outside of your salary?" asked Roswell.

"From three to five dollars a week."

"I should think they'd find you out."

"I don't let them. I'm pretty careful. Well, what shall we do this evening? There's a pretty good play at Niblo's. Suppose we go there."

"I haven't got money enough," said Roswell.

"Well, I'll pay for both to-night. You can pay another time."

"All right!" said Roswell, though he did not know when he should have money enough to return the favor. They crossed to Broadway, and walked leisurely to Niblo's Garden. The performance lasted till late, and it was after eleven when Roswell Crawford got into bed.

CHAPTER XVIII.

THE FIRST STEP.

To do Roswell Crawford justice, the idea of taking money from his employer had never occurred to him until the day when it was suggested to him by Ralph Graham. The suggestion came to him at an unfortunate time. He had always felt with a sense of bitter injustice that his services were poorly compensated, and that his employer was making money out of him. Yet he knew very well that there was no chance of an advance. Besides, he really felt the need of more money to keep up appearances equal to Ralph Graham, and some other not very creditable acquaintances that he had managed to pick up. So Roswell allowed Ralph's suggestion to recur to his mind with dangerous frequency. He was getting familiar with what had at first startled and shocked him.

But it was not at once that he brought his mind

to the point. He was not possessed of much courage, and could not help fearing that he would get himself into a scrape. It needed a little more urging on the part of Ralph.

"Well, Roswell," said Ralph, a few evenings after the conversation recorded in the last chapter, "when are you going to take me to the theatre?"

"I didn't know I was going to take you at all," said Roswell.

"Come, there's no use in crawling off that way. Didn't I take you to Niblo's last week?"

"Yes."

"And didn't you promise to take me some night in return?"

"I should like to do it well enough," said Roswell. "but I never have any money."

"You might have some if you chose."

"The way you mentioned?"

"Yes."

"I don't like to try it."

"Then you are foolish. It's what half the clerks do They have to."

"Do you think many do it?" said Roswell, irresolutely.

"To be sure they do," said Ralph, confidently

"But I am sure it would be found out."

"Not if you're careful."

"I shouldn't know how to go about it."

"Then I'll tell you. You're in the store alone some of the time, I suppose."

"Yes, when Mr. Baker and Mr. Jones are gone to dinner."

"Where is the money kept?"

"There are two drawers. The one that has the most money in it is kept locked, and Mr. Baker carries away the key with him. He leaves a few dollars in another drawer, but nothing could be taken from that drawer without being missed."

"Does he keep much money in the first drawer?"

"I expect so."

"Then," said Ralph, promptly, "you must manage to get into that."

"But how am I to do it?" asked Roswell. "Didn't I tell you that it was kept locked, and that Mr. Baker took the key?"

"I can't say you are very smart, Roswell," said Ralph, a little contemptuously.

"Tell me what you mean, then."

"What is easier than to get a key made that will fit the drawer? All you'll have to do. is to take an impression of the lock with sealing-wax, and carry i to a locksmith. He'll make you a key for two shillings."

"I don't know," said Roswell, undecidedly. "I don't quite like to do it."

"Do just as you please," said Ralph; "only if I carry you to the theatre I expect you to return the compliment."

"Well, I'll think of it," said Roswell.

"There is another way you can do," suggested Ralph, who was full of evil suggestions, and was perhaps the most dangerous counsellor that Roswell could have had at this time.

"What is it?"

"If you make any sales while you are alone you might forget to put the money into the drawer."

"Yes, I might do that."

"And ten to one Baker would never suspect. Of course he doesn't know every book he has in his store or the exact amount of stationery he keeps on hand."

"No, I suppose not."

"You might begin that way. There couldn't be any danger of detection."

This suggestion struck Roswell more favorably than the first, as it seemed safer. Without giving any decided answer, he suffered the thought to sink into his mind, and occupy his thoughts.

The next day when about the middle of the day Roswell found himself alone, a customer came in and bought a package of envelopes, paying twenty-five cents.

With a half-guilty feeling Roswell put this sum into his pocket.

"Mr. Baker will never miss a package of envelopes," he thought.

He sold two or three other articles, but the money received for these he put into the drawer. He did not dare to take too much at first. Indeed, he took a little credit to himself, so strangely had his ideas of honesty got warped, for not taking more when he might have done so as well as not.

Mr. Baker returned, and nothing was said. As might have been expected, he did not miss the small sum which Roswell had appropriated.

That evening Roswell bought a couple of cigars

with the money he had stolen (we might as well call things by their right names), and treated Ralph to one.

"There's a splendid play on at Wallack's," said he, suggestively.

"Perhaps we'll go to-morrow evening," said Roswell.

"That's the way to talk," said Ralph, looking keenly at Roswell. "Is there anything new with you?"

"Not particularly," said Roswell, coloring a little, for he did not care to own what he had done to his companion, though it was from him that he had received the advice.

The next day when Roswell was again alone, a lady entered the shop.

"Have you got La Fontaine's Fables in English?" she asked. "I have asked at half a dozen stores, but I can't find it. I am afraid it is out of print."

"Yes, I believe we have it," said Roswell.

He remembered one day when he was looking for a book he wanted to read, that he had come across a shop-worn copy of La Fontaine's Fables. It was on a back shelf, in an out of-the-way place. He looked for it, and found his memory had served him correctly.

"Here it is," he said, handing it down.

"I am very glad to get it," said the lady. How much will it be?"

"The regular price is a dollar and a quarter, but as this is a little shop-worn you may have it for a dollar."

"Very well."

The lady drew out a dollar bill from her purse, and handed it to Roswell.

He held it in his hand till she was fairly out of the door. Then the thought came into his mind, "Why should I not keep this money? Mr. Baker would never know. Probably he has quite forgotten that such a book was in his stock."

Besides, as the price of a ticket to the family circle at Wallack's was only thirty cents, this sum would carry in him and his friend, and there would be enough left for an ice-cream after they had got through.

The temptation was too much for poor Roswell. I call him poor, because I pity any boy who fool ishly yields to such a temptation for the sake of a temporary gratification.

Roswell put the money into his vest-pocket, and shortly afterwards Mr. Baker returned to the store.

"Have you sold anything, Roswell?" he inquired, on entering

"Yes, sir. I have sold a slate, a quire of note-paper, and one of Oliver Optic's books."

Roswell showed Mr. Baker the slate, on which, as required by his employer, he had kept a record of sales.

Mr. Baker made no remark, but appeared to think all was right.

So the afternoon passed away without any incident worthy of mention.

In the evening Roswell met Ralph Graham, as he had got into the habit of doing.

"Well, Roswell, I feel just like going to the theatre to-night," were his first words of salutation.

"Well, we'll go," said Roswell.

"Good! You've got money to buy the tickets, then?"

"Yes," said Roswell, with an air of importance. "What's the play?"

"It's a London play that's had a great run. Tom Hastings tells me it is splendid. You take me there to night, and I'll take you to the New York Circus some evening next week."

This arrangement was very satisfactory to Roswell, who had never visited the circus, and had a great desire to do so. At an early hour the boys went to the theatre, and succeeded in obtaining front seats in the family circle. Roswell managed to enjoy the play, although unpleasant thoughts of how the money was obtained by which the tickets were procured, would occasionally intrude upon him. But the fascination of the stage kept them from troubling him much.

When the performance was over, he suggested an ice-cream.

"With all my heart," said Ralph. "I feel warm and thirsty, and an ice-cream will cool my throat."

So they adjourned to a confectionery establishment nearly opposite, and Roswell, with an air of importance, called for the creams. They sat leisurely over them, and it was nearly half past eleven when Roswell got home.

"What keeps you out so late, Roswell?" asked his mother, anxiously, for she was still up.

"I was at the theatre." said Roswell

"Where did you get the money?"

"It's only thirty cents to the family circle," said Roswell, carelessly. "I'm tired, and will go right up to bed."

So he closed the discussion, not caring to answer many inquiries as to his evening's amusement. His outlay for tickets and for the ice-cream afterwards had just used up the money he had stolen, and all that he had to compensate for the loss of his integrity was a headache, occasioned by late hours, and the warm and confined atmosphere at the theatre.

CHAPTER XIX.

RICHARD HUNTER IS PROMOTED.

It was with eager impatience that Mark awaited the return of Richard Hunter, to communicate to him his good luck in securing a place. The thought that he had secured it by his own exertions gave him great satisfaction.

"I've got a place," were his first words, as Richard entered the house.

"Already?" asked Richard Hunter. "You have been quite smart, Mark. How did you manage to obtain it?"

Mark gave the particulars, which need not be repeated.

"What kind of a store is it?"

"A bookstore."

"What is the name of your employer?"

"Baker.'

"Baker's bookstore!" repeated Richard, turning

to Fosdick. "That is where our particular friend, Roswell Crawford, is employed."

"Yes," said Mark; "there's a boy there about sixteen or seventeen. I believe that is his name."

"I am not sure whether his being there will make it pleasant to you. Does he know that you are a friend of mine?"

"Yes," said Mark; "he inquired particularly about you, Mr. Hunter."

"He's very fond of me," said Dick; "I suppose he sent me his love."

"No," said Mark, smiling; "he didn't speak as if he loved you very much."

"He doesn't like me very much. I am afraid when he gets to be president I shan't stand much chance of an office. He didn't try to bully you, — did he?"

"He said he could get me sent off if I wasn't careful to please him."

"That sounds like Roswell."

'He talked as if he was one of the firm," said Mark; "but when Mr. Baker came in, he began to scold him for not dusting the books. After that I didn't think so much of what he said."

"It's a way he has," said Fosdick. "He don't like me much either, as I got a place that he was trying for."

"If he bullies you, just let me know," said Richard. "Perhaps I can stop it."

"I am not afraid," said Mark. "Mr. Baker is there most of the time, and he wouldn't dare to bully me before him."

Sunday morning came, — a day when the noisy streets were hushed, and the hum of business was stilled. Richard Hunter and Fosdick still attended the Sunday school, to which they had now belonged for over two years. They were still members of Mr. Greyson's class, and were much better informed in religious matters than formerly. Frequently — for they were favorite scholars with Mr. Greyson — he invited them home to dine at his handsome residence. Both boys were now perfectly self-possessed on such occasions. They knew how to behave at the table with perfect decorum, and no one would have judged from their dress, manners, or conversation, that they had not always been accustomed to the same style of living.

Mr. and Mrs Greyson noticed with pleasure the

great improvement in their protegés, and always welcomed them with kind hospitality But there was another member of the family who always looked forward with pleasure to seeing them. This was Ida, now a young lady of thirteen, who had from the first taken an especial fancy to Dick, as she always called him.

"Well, Mark," said Richard Hunter, on Sunday morning, "wouldn't you like to go to Sunday-school with me?"

"Yes," said Mark. "Mother always wanted me to go to Sunday school, but she was so poor that she could not dress me in suitable clothes."

"There is nothing to prevent your going now. We shall be ready in about half an hour."

At the appointed time the three set out. The distance was not great, the church being situated four blocks farther up town on Fifth Avenue. They chanced to meet Mr. Greyson on the church steps.

"Good-morning, Richard. Good-morning, Henry," he said. Then, glancing at Mark, "Who is your young friend?"

"His name is Mark Manton," said Richard "He is my ward."

"Indeed! I had not thought of you in the character of a guardian," said Mr. Greyson, smiling.

"I should like to have him enter one of the younger classes," said Richard.

"Certainly, I will gladly find a place for him. Perhaps you can take him in your class."

"In my class!" repeated Richard, in surprise.

"Yes, I thought I had mentioned to you that Mr. Benton was about to leave the city, and is obliged to give up his class. I would like to have you take it."

"But am I qualified to be a teacher?" asked Richard, who had never before thought of being invited to take a class.

"I think you have excellent qualifications for such a position. It speaks well for you, however, that you should feel a modest hesitation on the subject."

"I think Fosdick would make a better teacher than I."

"Oh, I intend to draft him into the service also. I shall ask him to take the next vacancy."

The class assigned to our friend Dick (we are sometimes tempted to call him by his old, familiar name) consisted of boys of from ten to eleven years of age. Among these Mark was placed. Although he had never before attended a Sunday school, his mother, who was an excellent woman, had given him considerable religious instruction, so that he was about as well advanced as the rest of the class.

Richard easily adapted himself to the new situation in which he was placed. He illustrated the lesson in a familiar and oftentimes quaint manner, so that he easily commanded the attention of the boys, who were surprised when the time came for the lesson to close.

"I am glad you are my teacher, Mr. Hunter," said one of the boys at the close of the service.

"Thank you," said Richard, who felt gratified at the compliment. "It's new business to me, but I hope I shall be able to interest you."

"Won't you come and dine with us?" asked Mr. Greyson, as they were leaving the church.

Richard Hunter hesitated.

"I don't know if Mark can find his way home," he said with hesitation.

"Yes, I can, Mr. Hunter," said Mark. "Don't trouble yourself about me."

"But I mean to have him come too," said Mr

Greyson. "Our table is a large one, as you know, and we can accommodate three as well as two."

"Do come, Dick," said Ida Greyson.

Richard was seldom able to resist a request preferred by Ida, and surrendered at discretion. So, as usual, Fosdick walked on with Mr. Greyson, this time with Mark beside him, while Richard walked with Ida.

"Who is that little boy, Dick?" asked the young lady.

"That's my ward, Miss Ida," said Richard.

"You don't mean to say you are his guardian, Dick?"

"Yes, I believe I am."

"Why," said the lively young lady, "I always thought guardians were old, and cross, and bald headed."

"I don't know but that description will suit me after a while," said Dick. "My hair has been coming out lately."

"Has it, really?" said Ida, who took this seriously. "I hope you won't be bald, I don't think you would look well."

"But I might wear a wig."

"I don't like wigs," said the young lady, decidedly. "If you were a lady now, you might wear a cap. How funny you'd look in a cap!" and she burst out into a peal of merry laughter.

"I think a cap would be more becoming to you," said Richard.

"Do you ever scold your ward?" asked Ida.

"No, he's a pretty good boy. He don't need it."

"Where did you get acquainted with him? Have you known him long?"

"He was taken sick at the door of our office one day. So I had him carried to my boarding-place, and took care of him till he got well."

"That was very good of you," said Ida, approvingly. "What did he use to do?"

"He was a match boy."

"Does he sell matches now?"

"No; he has got a place in a bookstore."

"What did you say his name was?"

"Mark."

"That's a pretty good name, but I don't like it so well as Dick."

"Thank you," said Richard. "I am glad you like my name."

At this moment they were passing the Fifth Avenue Hotel. Standing on the steps were two acquaintances of ours, Roswell Crawford and Ralph Graham. They had cigars in their mouths, and there was a swaggering air about them, which was not likely to prepossess any sensible person in their favor. They had not been to church, but had spent the morning in sauntering about the city, finally bringing up at the Fifth Avenue Hotel, where, posting themselves conspicuously on the steps, they watched the people passing by on their way from church.

Richard Hunter bowed to Roswell, as it was his rule never to be found wanting in politeness. Roswell was ill-mannered enough not to return the salutation.

"Who is that, Roswell?" asked Ralph Graham.

"It's a boot-black," said Roswell, sneeringly.

"What do you mean? I am speaking of that nice-looking young fellow that bowed to you just now."

"His name is Hunter. He used to be a boot-black, as I told you; but he's got up in the world, and now he's putting on airs."

"He seems to have got into good company, at any rate. He is walking with the daughter of Mr. Greyson, a rich merchant down town."

"He's got impudence enough for anything," sai Roswell, with a feeling of bitter envy which he could not conceal. "It really makes me sick to see him strutting about as if he were a gentleman's son."

"Like you," suggested Ralph, slyly; for he had already been informed by Roswell, on various occasions, that he was "a gentleman's son."

"Yes," said Roswell, "I'm a gentleman's son, if I'm not so lucky as some people. Did you see that small boy in front?"

"Walking with Mr. Greyson?"

"Yes, I suppose so."

"What of him?"

"That's our errand boy."

"Is it?" asked Ralph, in some surprise. "He seems to be one of the lucky kind too."

"He sold matches about the streets till a few weeks ago," said Roswell, spitefully.

"He sold them to some purpose, it seems, for he's evidently going home to dine with Mr. Greyson"

"Mr. Greyson seems to be very fond of low com pany. That's all I can say."

"When you and I get to be as rich as he is, we can choose our own company."

"I hope I shall choose better than he."

"Well, let's drop them," said Ralph, who was getting tired of the subject. "I must be getting home to dinner."

"So must I."

"Come round to my room, after dinner, and we'll have another smoke."

"Yes, I'll come round. I suppose mother'll be wanting me to go to church with her, but I've got tired of going to church."

CHAPTER XX

THE MADISON CLUB.

Two days afterwards, when Roswell as usual met his friend Ralph, the latter said, with an air of importance: —

"I've got news for you, Roswell."

"What is it?" inquired Roswell.

"You've been unanimously elected a member of our club."

"Your club?"

"Yes; didn't I ever mention it to you?"

"No."

"Well, I believe I didn't. You see I intended to propose your name as a member, and not feeling certain whether you would be elected, I thought I had better not mention it to you."

"What is the name of the club?" asked Roswell, eagerly.

"The Madison Club."

"What made you call it that?"

"Why, you see, there's one fellow in the club that lives on Madison Avenue, and we thought that would be an aristocratic name, so we chose it."

Roswell liked whatever was aristocratic, and the name pleased him.

"Did you say I was unanimously elected, Ralph?" he asked.

"Yes; I proposed your name at our meeting last night. It was on account of that, that I couldn't meet you as usual. But hereafter we can go together to the meetings."

"How many fellows belong?"

"Twenty. We don't mean to have more than twenty-five. We are quite particular whom we elect."

"Of course," said Roswell, in a tone of importance. "You wouldn't want a set of low fellows like that Dick Hunter."

"No. By the way, I've got somewhere your notification from the secretary. Here it is."

He drew from his pocket a note adorned with a large and elaborate seal, which Roswell, opening, found read as follows: —

"MADISON CLUB.

"MR. ROSWELL CRAWFORD.

"Sir: — I have the honor of informing you that at the last regular meeting of the Madison Club you were unanimously elected a member.

"Yours respectfully,

"JAMES TRACY."

This document Roswell read with much satisfaction. It sounded well to say that he was a member of the Madison Club, and his unanimous election could only be regarded as a high compliment.

"I will join," he said, pompously. "When is the next meeting?"

"Next Tuesday evening."

"Where does the society meet?"

In a room on Fourth Avenue. You can come round early, and we will go together."

"All right. What do you do at the meetings?"

"Well, we smoke, and tell stories, and have a good time. Generally there are some eatables provided. However, you'll know all about it, when you join. Oh, by the way, there's one thing I forgot to tell you," added Ralph. "There's an initiation fee of five dollars."

"A fee of five dollars!" repeated Roswell, soberly.

"Yes."

"What is it for?"

"To defray expenses, of course. There's the rent, and lights, and stationery, and the eatables. They always, I think, have an initiation fee at clubs."

"Are there any other expenses?"

"Not much. There's only a dollar a month. That isn't much."

"I don't know how I'm going to raise the five dollars," said Roswell, soberly. "I could manage the dollar a month afterwards."

"Oh, you'll think of some way," said Ralph.

"My mother wouldn't give it to me, so there's no use asking her."

"Why can't you pay it out of your extra wages?" said Ralph, significantly.

"I shouldn't dare to take such a large sum," said Roswell. "They would find me out."

"Not if you're careful."

"They don't keep but a few dollars in the drawer at one time."

"But didn't you tell me there was another drawer?"

"Yes; but that is always kept locked."

"Open it then."

"I have no key."

"Get one that will fit it then."

"I don't like to do that."

"Well, it's nothing to me," said Ralph, "only I should like to have you belong to the club, and you can't unless you are able to pay the initiation fee."

"I would like very much to belong," said Roswell, irresolutely.

"I know you would enjoy it. We have splendid times."

"I'll see what I can do to raise the money," said Roswell.

"That's the way to talk. You'll manage to get it some way"

It was a great temptation to Roswell. The more he thought of it, the more he thought he should like to say that he was a member of the Madison Club. He had a weak love of gentility, and he was persuaded that it would improve his social standing. But he did not wish to adopt the course recommended by Ralph if there was any other way of getting the money. He determined, therefore, first to make the effort to obtain the money from his mother on some pretext or other. By the time he reached home, which was at an earlier hour than usual, he had arranged his pretext.

"I am glad you are home early," said Mrs. Crawford.

"Yes, I thought I'd come home early to-night. Mother, I wish you'd let me have four dollars."

"What for, Roswell?"

"I want to buy a new hat. This one is getting shabby."

Roswell's plan was, if he could obtain the four dollars from his mother, to make up the extra dollar out of sales unaccounted for. As to the failure to buy the hat, he could tell his mother that he had lost the money, or make some other excuse. That thought did not trouble him much. But he was not destined to succeed.

"I am sorry you are dissatisfied with your hat, Roswell," said Mrs. Crawford, "for I cannot possibly spare you the money now."

"So you always say," grumbled Roswell.

"But it's true," said his mother. "I'm very short just now. The rent comes due in a few days, and I am trying hard to get together money enough to pay it."

"I thought you had money coming in from your lodgers."

"There's Mr. Bancroft hasn't paid me for six weeks, and I'm afraid I am going to lose his room-rent. "It's hard work for a woman to get along. Everybody takes advantage of her," said Mrs. Crawford, sighing.

"Can't you possibly let me have the money by Saturday, mother?"

"No, Roswell. Perhaps in a few weeks I can. But I don't think your hat looks bad. You can go and get it pressed if you wish."

But Roswell declared that wouldn't do, and left the room in an ill-humor. Instead of feeling for his mother, and wishing to help her, he was intent only upon his own selfish gratifications.

So much, then, was plain, — in his efforts to raise the money for the initiation fee at the club, he could not expect any help from his mother. He must rely upon other means.

Gradually Roswell came to the determination to follow the dangerous advice which had been proffered him by Ralph Graham. He could not bear to give up the project of belonging to the club, and was willing to commit a dishonest act rather than forego the opportunity.

He began to think now of the manner in which he could accomplish what he had in view. The next day when noon came he went round to the locked drawer, and, lighting a piece of sealing-wax which he had taken from one of the cases, he obtained a clear impression of the lock.

"I think that will do," thought Roswell.

At that moment a customer entered the store, and he hurried the stick of sealing-wax into his pocket.

When the store closed, Roswell went round to a locksmith, whose sign he remembered to have seen in Third Avenue.

He entered the shop with a guilty feeling at his heart, though he had a plausible story arranged for the occasion.

"I want a key made," he said, in a business-like manner; "one that will fit this lock."

Here he displayed the wax impression.

"What sort of a lock is it?" asked the locksmith, looking at it.

"It is a bureau drawer," said Roswell. "We have lost the key, and can't open it. So I took the impression in wax. How soon can you let me have it?"

"Are you in a hurry for it?"

"Yes; didn't I tell you we couldn't open the drawer?"

"Well, I'll try to let you have it by to-morrow night."

"That will do," said Roswell.

He left the locksmith's shop with mixed feelings of satisfaction and shame at the thought of the use to which he was intending to put the key. It was a great price he had determined to pay for the honor of belonging to the Madison Club.

CHAPTER XXI.

ROSWELL JOINS THE MADISON CLUB

It was not until Saturday night that Roswell obtained the key. The locksmith, like tradesmen and mechanics in general, kept putting him off, to Roswell's great annoyance.

As he did not get the key till Saturday night, of course there would be no opportunity of using it till Monday. The only time then was the hour in which Mr. Baker and Mr. Jones were absent, and Roswell was left alone. But to his great vexation, an old gentleman came in directly after Mr. Baker went out, and inquired for him.

"He's gone to dinner," said Roswell.

"I think I'll wait till he returns," said the visitor, coolly sitting down in Mr. Baker's arm-chair.

Roswell was in dismay, for this would of course prevent his using the key which he had taken so much trouble to obtain.

"Mr. Baker is always out a good while," said Roswell.

"Never mind, I can wait for him. I came in from the country this morning, and shall not need to start back till four."

"Perhaps," suggested Roswell, "you could go out and do the rest of your errands, and come back at two o'clock. Mr. Baker will be sure to be back then."

"Who told you I had any more errands to do?" asked the old gentleman, sharply.

"I thought you might have," said Roswell, somewhat confused.

"You are very considerate; but, as my business is over for the day, I will ask your permission to remain till my nephew returns."

So this was Mr. Baker's uncle, a shrewd old gentlemen, if he did live in the country.

"Certainly," said Roswell, but not with a very good grace, adding to himself; "there'll be no chance for me to get the money to-day. I hope the old fellow won't come round again to-morrow."

The next day was Tuesday. In the evening the club was to meet, so there was no time to lose.

Fortunately, as Roswell thought, the coast was clear.

"Suppose the key won't fit?" he thought with uneasiness.

It would have been lucky for Roswell if the key had not fitted. But it proved to fit exactly. Turning it in the lock, the drawer opened, and before him lay a pile of bills.

How much or how little there might be Roswell did not stop to examine. He knew that a customer might come in at any time, and he must do at once what he meant to do. At the top of the pile there was a five-dollar bill. He took it, slipped it hastily into his vest-pocket, relocked the drawer, and, walking away from it, began to dust the books upon the counter.

He felt that he had taken the decisive step. He was supplied with the necessary money to pay the initiation fee. The question was, would Mr. Baker find it out?

Suppose he should, how would it be possible to evade suspicion, or to throw it upon some one else?

"If I could make him think it was the match

boy," thought Roswell, "I should be ki.ling two birds with one stone. I must see what can be done."

When Mr. Baker returned, Roswell feared he would gc to the drawer, but he did not seem inclined to do this.

He just entered the store, and said, "Mr. Jones, I am obliged to go over to Brooklyn on a little business, and I may not be back this afternoon."

"Very well, sir," said Mr. Jones.

Roswell breathed freer after he had left the shop. It had occurred to him as possible that if the money were missed, he might be searched, in which case the key and the bill in his pocket would be enough to convict him. Now he should not see Mr. Baker again till the next day probably, when the money would be disposed of.

Mr. Baker, as he anticipated, did not return from Brooklyn before Roswell left the store.

Roswell snatched a hasty supper, and went over to his friend, Ralph Graham's room, immediately afterwards.

"Glad to see you, Roswell," said Ralph; "are you coming to the club with me to-night?"

"Yes," said Roswell.

"Have you got the five dollars?"

"Yes."

"How did you manage it?"

"Oh, I contrived to get it," said Roswell, who did not like to confess in what way he had secured possession of the money.

"Well, it's all right, as long as you've got it. I was afraid you wouldn't succeed."

"So was I," said Roswell. "I had hard work of it. What time do the club meetings begin?" he asked.

"At eight o'clock, but I generally go round about half an hour before. Generally, some of the fellows are there, and we can have a social chat. I guess we'll go round at half-past seven, and that will give me a chance to introduce you to some of the members before the meeting begins."

"I should like that," said Roswell.

In a short time the boys set out. They paused before a small house on Fourth Avenue, and rang the bell. The summons was answered by a colored man.

"Any members of the club upstairs?" inquired Ralph.

"Yes, sir," said the attendant. "There's Mr. Tracy, Mr. Wilmot, and Mr. Burgess."

"Very well, I'll go up."

"Jackson," said Ralph, "this gentleman is Mr. Crawford, a new member."

"Glad to make your acquaintance, sir," said Jackson.

"Thank you," said Roswell.

"Jackson takes care of the club-room," explained Ralph, "and is in attendance to admit the members on club nights. Now let us go upstairs."

They went up one flight of stairs, and opened the door of a back room.

It was not a very imposing-looking apartment, being only about twenty feet square, the floor covered with a faded carpet, while the furniture was not particularly sumptuous. At one end of the room was a table, behind which were two arm-chairs.

"That is where the president and secretary sit," said Ralph.

There were already three or four youths in the room. One of them came forward and offered his hand to Ralph.

"How are you, Graham?" he said.

"How are you, Tracy?" returned Ralph "This is Mr. Crawford, who was elected a member at our last meeting. Roswell, this is Mr Tracy, our secretary"

"I am glad to see you, Mr. Crawford," said Tracy. "I hope you received the notification of your election which I sent you."

"Yes," said Roswell. "I am much obliged to you."

"I hope you intend to accept."

"It will give me great pleasure," said Roswell. "You must have very pleasant meetings."

"I hope you will find them pleasant. By the way, here is our president, Mr. Brandon. Brandon, let me introduce you to a new member of our society, Mr. Crawford."

The president, who was a tall young man of eighteen, bowed graciously to Roswell.

"Mr. Crawford," said he, "allow me, in the name of the society, to bid you welcome to our gay and festive meetings. We are a band of good fellows, who like to meet together and have a social time. We are proud to receive you into our ranks."

"And I am very glad to belong," said Roswell,

who felt highly pleased at the cordial manner in which he was received.

"You'd better go to the secretary, and enter your name in the books of the club," suggested Ralph. "You can pay him the five dollars at the same time. Here, Tracy, Mr. Crawford wants to enroll his name."

"All right," said Tracy; "walk this way if you please, Mr. Crawford."

Roswell wrote down his name, residence, and the store where he was employed.

"I see, Mr. Crawford, you are engaged in literary pursuits," said the secretary.

"Yes, for the present," said Roswell. "I don't think I shall remain long, as the book business doesn't give me scope enough; but I shall not leave at present, as it might inconvenience Mr. Baker. What is your initiation fee?"

"Five dollars."

"I happen to have the money with me, I believe," said Roswell. "Here it is"

"Thank you; that is right. I will enter you as paid The monthly assessments are one dollar, as perhaps Graham told you."

"Yes, I think he mentioned it. It is quite reasonable, I think," said Roswell, in a tone which seemed to indicate that he was never at a loss for money.

"Yes, I think so, considering our expenses. You see we have to pay for the room; then we pay Jackson's wages, and there are cigars, etc., for the use of the members. Have you ever before belonged to a club?"

"No," said Roswell. "I have always declined hitherto (he had never before received an invitation) but I was so much pleased with what I heard of th Madison Club from my friend Graham, that I determined to join. I am glad that you are particular whom you admit as members of the club."

"Oh, yes, we are very exclusive," said Tracy. "We are not willing to admit anybody and everybody."

Meanwhile there had been numerous arrivals, until probably nearly all the members of the club were present.

"Order, gentlemen!" said the president, assuming the chair, and striking the table at the same time "The club will please come to order."

There was a momentary confusion, but at length the members settled into their seats, and silence prevailed. Roswell Crawford took a seat beside Ralph Graham.

CHAPTER XXII.

A CLUB NIGHT.

"The secretary will read the journal of the last meeting," said President Brandon.

Tracy rose, and read a brief report, which was accepted, according to form.

"Is there any business to come before the club?" inquired the president.

"I would like to nominate a friend of mine as a member of the club," said Burgess.

"What's his name?" inquired a member.

"Henry Drayton."

"Will Mr. Burgess give some account of his friend, so that the members can vote intelligently on his election?" requested Brandon.

"He's a jolly sort of fellow, and a good singer," said Burgess. "He'll help make our meetings lively. He's about my age —"

"In his second childhood," suggested Wilmot.

This produced a laugh at the expense of Burgess, who took it good-naturedly.

"Has he got five dollars?" inquired another member.

"His father is a rich man," said Burgess. "There will be no fear about his not paying his assessments."

"That's the principal thing," said Wilmot. "I second the nomination."

A vote was taken which was unanimously affirmative.

"Mr. Drayton is unanimously elected a member of the Madison Club," announced the president. "Notification will be duly sent him by the secretary. Is there any other business to come before the club?"

As there appeared to be none, Brandon added, "Then we will proceed to the more agreeable duties which have brought us hither."

He rang a small bell.

Jackson answered the summons.

"Jackson, is the punch ready?" inquired the president.

"Yes, sir," said Jackson.

"Then bring it in. I appoint Wilmot and Burgess to lend you the necessary aid."

A large flagon of hot whiskey punch was brought in and placed on a table. Glasses were produced from a closet in the corner of the room, and it was served out to the members.

"How do you like it, Roswell?" inquired Ralph Graham.

"It's — rather strong," said Roswell, coughing.

"Oh, you'll soon be used to it. The fellows will begin to be jolly after they've drunk a glass or two."

"Do they ever get tight?" whispered Roswell.

"A little lively, — that's all."

The effect predicted soon followed.

"Wilmot, give us a song," said Burgess.

"What will you have?" said Wilmot, whose flushed face showed that the punch had begun to affect him.

"Oh, you can give us an air from one of the operas."

"Villikens and his Dinah?" suggested Tracy.

"Very good." said Wilmot.

Wilmot was one of those, who, with no voice or

musical ear, are under the delusion that they are admirable singers. He executed the song in his usual style, and was rewarded with vociferous applause, which appeared to gratify him.

"Gentleman," he said, laying his hand upon his heart, "I am deeply grateful for your kind appreciation of my —"

"Admirable singing," suggested Dunbar.

"Of my admirable singing," repeated Wilmot, gravely.

This speech was naturally followed by an outburst of laughter. Wilmot looked around him in grave surprise.

"I don't see what you fellows are laughing at," he said, "unless you're all drunk."

He sat down amid a round of applause, evidently puzzled to understand the effect of his words.

After this, David Green arose, and rehearsed amid great applause a stump speech which he had heard at some minstrel entertainment which he had attended.

"How do you like it, Roswell?" again inquired Ralph Graham.

"It's splendid," said Roswell, enthusiastically.

"Are you glad you joined?"

"Yes; I wouldn't have missed it for a good deal."

"I knew you'd say so. Have your glass filled. Here Jackson, fill this gentleman's glass."

Roswell was beginning to feel a little light-headed; but the punch had excited him, and he had become in a degree reckless of consequences. So he made no opposition to the proposal, but held out his glass, which was soon returned to him filled to the brim.

"Speech from the new member!" called Dunbar, after a while.

"Yes, speech, speech!"

All eyes were turned towards Roswell.

"You'd better say something," said Ralph.

Roswell rose to his feet, but found it necessary to hold on to his chair for support.

"Mr. President," commenced Roswell, gazing about him in a vacant way, "this is a great occasion."

"Of course it is," said Burgess.

"We are assembled to-night —"

"So we are. Bright boy!" said David Green

"I am a gentleman's son," continued Roswell.

"What's the gentleman's name?" interrupted Wilmot.

"And I think it's a shame that I should only be paid six dollars a week for my services."

"Bring your employer here, and we'll lynch him," said Tracy. "Such mean treatment of a member of the Madison Club should meet with the severest punishment. Go ahead."

"I don't think I've got anything more to say," said Roswell. "As my head doesn't feel just right, I'll sit down."

There was a round of applause, and Wilmot arose.

"Mr. President," he said, gravely, "I have been very much impressed with the remarks of the gentleman who has just sat down. They do equal credit to his head and his heart. His reference to his salary was most touching. If you will allow me, I will pause a moment and wipe away an unbidden tear." (Here amid laughter and applause, Wilmot made an imposing demonstration with a large handkerchief. He then proceeded.) "Excuse my emotion, gentlemen. I merely arose to make the motion that the gentleman should furnish us a copy of his remarks, that they may be engrossed on parchment, and a copy sent to the principal libraries in Europe and America."

Roswell was hardly in a condition to understand that fun was being made of him, but listened soberly, sipping from time to time from his glass.

"The motion is not in order," said Brandon. "The hour for business has gone by."

The punch was now removed, and cards were produced. The remainder of the evening was spent in playing euchre and other games. Roswell took a hand, but found he was too dizzy to play correctly, and for the remainder of the evening contented himself with looking on. Small sums were staked among some of the players, and thus a taste for gambling was fostered which might hereafter lead to moral shipwreck and ruin.

This was the way in which the members of the Madison Club spent their evenings, — a very poor way, as my young readers will readily acknowledge. I heartily approve of societies organized by young people for debate and mutual improvement. They are oftentimes productive of great good. Some of our distinguished men date their first impulse to improve and advance themselves to their connection with such a society. But the Madison Club had no salutary object in view. It was adapted to inspire a taste for gambling and drinking, and the money spent by the members to sustain it was worse than wasted.

Roswell, however. who would have found nothing to interest or attract him in a Debating Society, was very favorably impressed by what he had seen of the Madison Club. He got an erroneous impression that it was likely to introduce him into the society of gentlemen, and his aristocratic predilections were, as we know, one of Roswell's hobbies.

It was about eleven when the club broke up its meeting. Previous to this there was a personal diffi culty between Wilmot and Tracy, which resulted in a rough-and-tumble fight, in which Wilmot got the worst of it. How the quarrel arose no one could remember,— the principals least of all. At last they were reconciled, and were persuaded to shake hands.

They issued into the street, a noisy throng. Roswell's head ached. the punch, to which he was not accustomed, having affected him in this way. Besides this he felt a little dizzy.

"I wish you'd come home with me, Ralph," he said to his friend. "I don't feel quite right."

"Oh, you'll feel all right to-morrow. Your head will become as strong as mine after a while. I'm as cool as a cucumber."

"It's rather late, isn't it?" asked Roswell.

"Hark, there's the clock striking. I'll count the strokes. Eleven o'clock!" he said, after counting. "That isn't very late."

Ralph accompanied Roswell to the door of his mother's house in Clinton Place.

"Good-night, old fellow!" he said. "You'll be all right in the morning.'

"Good-night," said Roswell.

He crept up to bed, but his brain was excited by the punch he had drank, and it was only after tossing about for two hours that he at length sank into a troubled sleep.

CHAPTER XXIII.

WHO WAS THE THIEF?

WHEN Roswell rose the next morning he felt cross and out of sorts. His head still ached a little, and he wished he were not obliged to go to the store. But it was out of the question to remain at home, so he started about half an hour after the usual time, and of course arrived late.

"You are late this morning," said Mr. Baker. "You must be more particular about being here in good season."

Roswell muttered something about not feeling quite well.

Putting his hand into his pocket by chance, his fingers came in contact with the key which he had made to open the cash drawer. Just as he was passing Mark, he drew it out and let it drop into the side-pocket of his jacket. So, if suspicion were excited, the key would be found on Mark, not on him

The critical moment came sooner than he had anticipated.

A Mr. Gay, one of the regular customers of the bookstore, entered a few minutes later.

"Good-morning, Mr. Baker," he said. "Have you got a 'Tribune' this morning?"

"Yes, here is one. By the way, you are just the man I wanted to see."

"Indeed, I feel complimented."

"Wait till you hear what I am going to say. You bought a copy of 'Corinne' here on Monday?"

"Yes."

"And handed me a five-dollar bill on the Park Bank?"

"Yes."

"Well, I find the bill was a skilfully executed counterfeit."

"Indeed! I didn't examine it very closely. But I know where I took it, and will give you a good bill in exchange for it."

"I locked it up lest it should get out," said Mr. Baker.

He went to the drawer which Roswell had opened

Roswell listened to this conversation with dismay

He realized that he was in a tight place, for it was undoubtedly the five-dollar counterfeit which he had taken, and paid to the Secretary of the Madison Club. He awaited nervously the result of Mr. Baker's examination.

"Don't you find it?" asked Mr. Gay.

"It is very strange," said Mr. Baker. "I placed it at the top of a pile of bills, and now it is gone."

"Look through the pile. Perhaps your memory is at fault," said Mr. Gay.

Mr. Baker did so.

"No," he said, "the bill has disappeared."

"Do you miss anything else?"

"No. The money is just five dollars short."

"Perhaps you forget yourself, and paid it away to a customer."

"Impossible; I always make change out of this drawer."

"Well, when you find it, I will make it right. I am in a hurry this morning."

Mr. Gay went out.

"Has any one been to this drawer?" inquired Mr. Baker, abruptly.

"You always keep it locked, — do you not?" said Mr. Jones.

"And keep the key myself. Yes."

"Then I don't see how it could have been opened."

"There was nothing peculiar about the lock. There might easily be another key to fit it."

"I hope you don't suspect me, Mr. Baker?"

"No, Mr. Jones, you have been with me five years, and I have perfect confidence in you."

"Thank you, sir."

"I hope you don't suspect me, sir," said Roswell, boldly. "I am willing to turn my pockets inside-out, to show that I have no key that will fit the lock."

"Very well. You may do so."

Roswell turned his pockets inside-out, but of course no key was found.

"How lucky I got rid of it!" he thought.

"Now it's your turn, Mark," he said.

"I'm perfectly willing," said Mark, promptly.

He put his hand into his pocket, and, to his unutterable astonishment and dismay, drew out a key.

"I didn't know I had this in my pocket," he said, startled.

"Hand me that key," said Mr. Baker, sternly.

Mark handed it to him mechanically.

Mr. Baker went behind the counter, and fitted the key in the lock. It proved to open the drawer with ease.

"Where did you get this key?" he said.

"I didn't know I had it, sir," said Mark, earnestly. "I hope you will believe me."

"I don't understand how you can hope anything of the kind. It seems very clear that you have been at my drawer, and taken the missing money. When did you take it?"

"I have never opened the drawer, nor taken your money," said Mark, in a firm voice, though his cheek was pale, and his look was troubled.

"I am sorry to say that I do not believe you," said Mr. Baker, coldly. "Once more, when did you take the five dollars?"

"I did not take it at all, sir."

"Have you lent the key to any one?"

"No, sir. I did not know I had it."

"I don't know what to do in the matter," said the

bookseller, turning to Mr. Jones, his assistant. "It seems clear to me that the boy took the missing bill."

"I am afraid so," said Jones, who was a kind-hearted man, and pitied Mark. "But I don't know when he could have had the chance. He is never left alone in the store."

"Roswell," said Mr. Baker, "have you left Mark alone in the store at any time within two or three days?"

Roswell saw the point of the inquiry, and determined, as a measure of safety, to add falsehood to his former offence.

"Yes, sir," he said, in an apologetic tone, "I left him in the store for two or three minutes yesterday."

"Why did you leave him? Did you go out of the store?"

"Yes, sir. A friend was passing, and I went out to speak to him. I don't think I stayed more than two or three minutes."

"And Mark was left alone in the store?"

"Yes, sir I had no idea that any harm would come of it."

Mark looked intently at Roswell when he uttered this falsehood.

"You had better confess, Mark, that you took the money when Roswell was out of the store," said his employer. "If you make a full confession, I will be as lenient with you as I can, considering your youth."

"Mr. Baker," said Mark, quietly, more at his ease now, since he began to understand that there was a plot against him, "I cannot confess what is not true. I don't know what Roswell means by what he has just said, but I was not left alone in the store for a moment all day yesterday, nor did Roswell go out to speak to a friend while I was about."

"There seems to be a conflict of evidence here," said Mr. Baker.

"I hope the word of a gentleman's son is worth more than that of a match boy," said Roswell, haughtily.

"To whom do you refer, when you speak of a match boy?"

"To *him*," said Roswell, pointing to Mark. "He used to be a vagabond boy about the streets.

selling matches, and sleeping anywhere he could No wonder he steals."

"I never stole in my life," said Mark, indignantly. "It is true that I sold matches about the streets, and I should have been doing it now, if it had not been for my meeting with kind friends."

"As to his having been a match boy, that has no bearing upon the question," said Mr. Baker. "It is the discovery of the key in his pocket that throws the gravest suspicion upon him. I must see his friends, and inquire into the matter."

"Of course they will stand by him," said Roswell.

"We may get some light thrown upon his possession of the key, at any rate, and can judge for ourselves."

"I shall keep you employed until this matter is investigated," said Mr. Baker to Mark. "Here is a parcel of books to be carried to Twenty-Seventh Street. Come back as soon as they are delivered."

Mark went out with a heavy heart, for it troubled him to think he was under suspicion. Theft, too, he had always despised. He wondered if Richard Hunter would believe him guilty. He could not bear to think that so kind a friend should think so ill of him

But Mark's vindication was not long in coming. He had been out scarcely ten minutes when Roswell, on looking up, saw to his dismay Tracy, the secretary of the Madison Club, entering the store. His heart misgave him as to the nature of the business on which he had probably come.

He went forward hastily to meet him.

"How are you, Crawford?" said Tracy.

"Pretty well. I am very busy now. I will see you, after the store closes, anywhere you please."

"Oh," said Tracy, in a voice loud enough for Mr. Baker to hear, "it won't take a minute. The bill you gave me last night was a bad one. Of course you didn't know it."

Roswell turned red and pale, and hoped Mr. Baker did not hear. But Mr. Baker had caught the words, and came forward.

"Show me the bill, if you please, young gentleman," he said. "I have a good reason for asking"

"Certainly, sir," said Tracy, rather surprised "Here it is."

A moment's glance satisfied Mr. Baker that it was the missing bill.

"Did Roswell pay you this bill?" he asked.

"Yes, sir."

"For what did he owe it?"

"I am the secretary of the Madison Club, and this was paid as the entrance fee."

"I recognize the bill," said Mr. Baker. "I will take it, if you please, and you can look to him for another."

"Very well," said Tracy, puzzled by the words, the motive of which he did not understand.

"Perhaps you will explain this," said Mr. Baker, turning to Roswell. "It seems that you took this bill."

Roswell's cofidence deserted him, and he stood pale and downcast.

"The key I presume, belonged to you."

"Yes, sir," he ejaculated, with difficulty.

"And you dropped it into Mark's pocket, — thus meanly trying to implicate him in a theft which you had yourself committed."

Roswell was silent.

"Have you taken money before?"

"I never opened the drawer but once."

"That was not my question. Make a full confession, and I will not have you arrested, but shall require you to make restitution of all the sums you have stolen. I shall not include this bill, as it is now returned to my possession. Here is a piece of paper. Write down the items."

Roswell did so. They footed up a little over six dollars.

Mr. Baker examined it.

"Is this all?" he said.

"Yes, sir."

"Half a week's wages are due you, I will therefore deduct three dollars from this amount. The remainder I shall expect you to refund. I shall have no further occasion for your services."

Roswell took his cap, and was about to leave the store.

"Wait a few minutes. You have tried to implicate Mark in your theft. You must wait till his return, and apologize to him for what you have attempted to do."

"Must I do this?" asked Roswell, ruefully.

"You must," said Mr. Baker, firmly.

When Mark came in, and was told how he had been cleared of suspicion, he felt very happy. Roswell made the apology dictated to him, with a very bad grace, and then was permitted to leave the store.

At home he tried to hide the circumstances attending his discharge from his mother and his cousin; but the necessity of refunding the money made that impossible.

It was only a few days afterwards that Mrs. Crawford received a letter, informing her of the death of a brother in Illinois, and that he had left her a small house and farm. She had found it so hard a struggle for a livelihood in the city, that she decided to remove thither, greatly to Roswell's disgust, who did not wish to be immured in the country. But his wishes could not be gratified, and, sulky and discontented, he was obliged to leave the choice society of the Madison Club, and the attractions of New York, for the quiet of a country town. Let us hope that, away from the influences of the city, his character may be improved, and become more manly and self-reliant. It is only just to say that he was led to appropriate what did not belong to him, by the desire to gratify his vanity, and through the influence of a bad adviser. If he can ever forget that he is "the son of a gentleman," I shall have some hopes for him

CHAPTER XXIV.

AN EXCURSION TO FORT HAMILTON.

TOWARDS the close of May there was a general holiday, occasioned by the arrival of a distinguished stranger in the city. All the stores were to be closed, there was to be a turnout of the military, and a long procession. Among those released from duty were our three friends, Fosdick, Richard Hunter, and his ward Mark.

"Well, Dick, what are you going to do to-morrow?" inquired Fosdick, on the evening previous.

"I was expecting an invitation to ride in a barouche with the mayor," said Richard; "but probably he forgot my address and couldn't send it. On the whole I'm glad of it, being rather bashful and not used to popular enthusiasm."

"Shall you go out and see the procession?" continued Fosdick.

"No," said Dick; "I have been thinking of another plan, which I think will be pleasanter."

"What is it?"

"It's a good while since we took an excursion. Suppose we go to Fort Hamilton to-morrow."

"I should like that," said Fosdick. "I was never there. How do we get there?"

"Cross over Fulton Ferry to Brooklyn, and there we might take the cars to Fort Hamilton. It's seven or eight miles out there."

"Why do you say 'might' take the cars?"

"Because the cars will be crowded with excursionists, and I have been thinking we might hire a carriage on the Brooklyn side, and ride out there in style. It'll cost more money, but we don't often take a holiday, and we can afford it for once. What you do say, Mark?"

"Do you mean me to go?" asked Mark, eagerly.

"Of course I do. Do you think your guardian would trust you to remain in the city alone?"

"I go in for your plan, Dick," said Fosdick "What time do you want to start?"

"About half-past nine o'clock. That will give us plenty of time to go. Then, after exploring the fort, we can get dinner at the hotel, and drive where we please afterwards. I suppose there is sea-bathing near by."

Dick's idea was unanimously approved, and by no one more than by Mark. Holidays had been few and far between with him, and he anticipated the excursion with the most eager delight. He was only afraid that the weather would prove unpropitious. He was up at four, looking out of the window; but the skies were clear, and soon the sun came out with full radiance, dissipating the night-shadows, and promising a glorious day.

Breakfast was later than usual, as people like to indulge themselves in a little longer sleep on Sundays and holidays; but it was over by half-past eight, and within a few minutes from that time the three had taken the cars to Fulton Ferry.

In about half an hour the ferry was reached, and, passing through, the party went on board the boat. They had scarcely done so, when an exclamation of surprise was heard, proceeding from feminine lips, and Dick heard himself called by name.

"Why, Mr. Hunter, this is an unexpected pleasure. I am *so* glad to have met you."

Turning his head, Dick recognized Mr. and Mrs. Clifton. Both had been fellow-boarders with him in Bleecker Street. The latter will be remembered by the readers of "Fame and Fortune" as Miss Peyton. When close upon the verge of old-maidenhood she had been married, for the sake of a few thousand dollars which she possessed, by Mr. Clifton, a clerk on a small salary, in constant pecuniary difficulties. With a portion of his wife's money he had purchased a partnership in a dry-goods store on Eighth Avenue; but the remainder of her money Mrs. Clifton had been prudent enough to have settled upon herself.

Mrs. Clifton still wore the same ringlets, and exhibited the same youthful vivacity which had characterized her when an inmate of Mrs. Browning's boarding-house, and only owned to being twenty-four, though she looked full ten years older.

"How d'e do, Hunter?" drawled Mr. Clifton, upon whose arm his wife was leaning.

"Very well, thank you," said Dick. "I see Mrs. Clifton is as fascinating as ever."

"O you wicked flatterer!" said Mrs. Clifton shaking her ringlets, and tapping Dick on the shoulder with her fan. "And here is Mr. Fosdick too, I declare. How do you do, Mr. Fosdick?"

"Quite well, thank you, Mrs. Clifton."

"I declare I've a great mind to scold you for not coming round to see us. I should so much like to hear you sing again."

"My friend hasn't sung since your marriage. Mrs. Clifton," said Dick. "He took it very much to heart. I don't think he has forgiven Clifton yet for cutting him out."

"Mr. Hunter is speaking for himself," said Fosdick, smiling. "He has sung as little as I have."

"Yes, but for another reason," said Dick. "I did not think it right to run the risk of driving away the boarders; so, out of regard to my landlady, I repressed my natural tendency to warble."

"I see you're just as bad as ever," said Mrs. Clifton, in excellent spirits. "But really you must come round and see us. We are boarding in West Sixteenth Street, between Eighth and Ninth Avenues."

"If your husband will promise not to be jealous" said Dick

"I'm not subject to that complaint," said Clifton, coolly "Got a cigar about you, Hunter?"

"No. I don't smoke."

"No, don't you though? I couldn't get along without it. It's my great comfort."

"Yes, he's always smoking," said Mrs. Clifton, with some asperity. "Our rooms are so full of tobacco smoke, that I don't know but some of my friends will begin to think I smoke myself."

"A man must have some pleasure," said Clifton, not appearing to be much discomposed by his wife's remarks.

It may be mentioned that although Mrs. Clifton was always gay and vivacious in company, there were times when she could display considerable ill-temper, as her husband frequently had occasion to know. Among the sources of difficulty and disagreement was that portion of Mrs. Clifton's fortune which had been settled upon herself, and of which she was never willing to allow her husband the use of a single dollar. In this, however, she had some justification, as he was naturally a spendthrift, and, if placed in his hands, it would soon have melted away.

"Where are you going, Mr. Hunter?" inquired Mrs Clifton, after a pause.

"Fosdick and I have planned to take a carriage and ride to Fort Hamilton."

"Delightful!" said Mrs. Clifton. "Why can't we go too, Mr. Clifton?"

"Why, to tell the plain truth," said her husband "I haven't got money enough with me. If you'll pay for the carriage, I'm willing to go."

Mrs. Clifton hesitated. She had money enough with her, but was not inclined to spend it. Still the prospect of making a joint excursion with Richard Hunter and Fosdick was attractive, and she inquired: —

"How much will it cost?"

"About five dollars probably."

"Then I think we'll go," she said, "that is, if our company would not be disagreeable to Mr. Hunter."

"On the contrary," said Dick. "We will get separate carriages, but I will invite you both to dine with us after visiting the fort."

Mr. Clifton brightened up at this, and straightway became more social and cheerful.

"Mrs. Clifton," said Richard Hunter, "I believe I haven't yet introduced you to my ward."

"Is that your ward?" inquired the lady, looking towards Mark. "What is his name?"

"Mark Manton."

"How do you like your guardian?" inquired Mrs. Clifton.

"Very much," said Mark, smiling.

"Then I won't expose him," said Mrs. Clifton. "We used to be great friends before I married."

"Since that sad event I have never recovered my spirits," said Dick. "Mark will tell you what a poor appetite I have."

"Is that true, Mark?" asked the lady.

"I don't think it's *very* poor," said Mark, with a smile.

Probably my readers will not consider this conversation very brilliant; but Mrs. Clifton was a silly woman, who was fond of attention, and was incapable of talking sensibly. Richard would have preferred not to have her husband or herself in the company, but, finding it inevitable, submitted to it with as good a grace as possible.

Carriages were secured at a neighboring stable,

and the two parties started. The drive was found to be very pleasant, particularly the latter portion, when a fresh breeze from the sea made the air delightfully cool. As they drove up beside the fort, they heard the band within, playing a march, and, giving their horses in charge, they were soon exploring the interior. The view from the ramparts proved to be fine, commanding a good view of the harbor and the city of New York, nearly eight miles distant to the north.

"It is a charming view," said Mrs. Clifton, with girlish enthusiasm.

"I know what will be more charming," said her husband.

"What is it?"

"A prospect of the dinner-table. I feel awfully hungry."

"Mr. Clifton never thinks of anything but eating," said his wife.

"By Jove! you can do your share at that," retorted her husband not very gallantly. "You'd ought to see her eat, Hunter."

"I don't eat more than a little bird," said Mrs Clifton, affectedly. "I appeal to Mr. Hunter."

"If any little bird ate as much as you, he'd be sure to die of *dyspepsy*," said her husband. If the word in italics is incorrectly spelled, I am not responsible, as that is the way Mr Clifton pronounced it.

"I confess the ride has given me an appetite also," said Dick. "Suppose we go round to the hotel, and order dinner."

They were soon seated round a bountifully spread dinner-table, to which the whole party, not excepting Mrs. Clifton, did excellent justice. It will not be necessary or profitable to repeat the conversation which seasoned the repast, as, out of deference to Mrs. Clifton's taste, none of the party ventured upon any sensible remarks.

After dinner they extended their drive, and then parted, as Mr. and Mrs. Clifton decided to make a call upon some friends living in the neighborhood.

About four o'clock Richard Hunter and his friends started on their return home. They had about reached the Brooklyn city line, when Fosdick suddenly exclaimed: —

"Dick, there's a carriage overturned a little ways ahead of us. Do you see it?"

Looking in the direction indicated, Dick saw that Fosdick was correct.

"Let us hurry on," he said. "Perhaps we may be able to render some assistance."

Coming up, they found that a wheel had come off, and a gentleman of middle age was leaning against a tree with an expression of pain upon his features. while a boy of about seventeen was holding the horse.

"Frank Whitney!" exclaimed Dick, in joyful recognition.

To Frank Whitney Dick was indebted for the original impulse which led him to resolve upon gaining a respectable position in society, as will be remembered by the readers of "Ragged Dick;" and for this he had always felt grateful.

"Dick!" exclaimed Frank, in equal surprise. "I am really glad to see you. You are a friend in need."

"Tell me what has happened."

"The wheel of our carriage came off, as you see and my uncle was pitched out with considerable violence, and has sprained his ankle badly. I was wondering what to do, when luckily you came up."

"Tell me how I can help you," said Dick, promptly, "and I will do so."

"We are stopping at the house of a friend in Brooklyn. If you will give my uncle a seat in your carryall, for he is unable to walk, and carry him there, it will be a great favor. I will remain and attend to the horse and carriage."

"With pleasure, Frank. Are you going to remain in this neighborhood long?"

"I shall try to gain admission to the sophomore class of Columbia College this summer, and shall then live in New York, where I hope to see you often. I intended to enter last year, but decided for some reasons to delay a year. However, if I am admitted to advanced standing, I shall lose nothing. Give me your address, and I will call on you very soon."

"I am afraid I shall inconvenience you," said Mr. Whitney.

"Not at all," said Dick, promptly. "We have plenty of room, and I shall be glad to have an opportunity of obliging one to whom I am indebted for past kindness."

Mr. Whitney was assisted into the carriage, and

they resumed their drive, deviating from their course somewhat, in order to leave him at the house of the friend with whom he was stopping.

"I am very glad to have met Frank again," thought Dick: "I always liked him."

CHAPTER XXV.

AN IMPORTANT DISCOVERY.

MARK remained in the bookstore on the same footing as before. He was not old enough to succeed to Roswell's vacant place, but Mr. Baker, as a mark of his satisfaction with him, and partly also to compensate for the temporary suspicions which he had entertained of his honesty, advanced his wages a dollar a week. He therefore now received four dollars, which yielded him no little satisfaction, as it enabled him to pay a larger share of his expenses.

They were all seated in Richard Hunter's pleasant room in St. Mark's Place one evening, when Dick said suddenly: —

"Oh, by the way, Fosdick, I forgot to tell you that I had a letter from Mr. Bates to-day."

"Did you? What does he say?"

"I will read it to you."

Richard drew the letter from the envelope, and read as follows: —

"MY DEAR MR. HUNTER: — I have received your letter, reporting that you have as yet obtained no trace of my unfortunate grandson, John Talbot. I thank you sincerely for your kind and persistent efforts. I fear that he may have left New York, possibly in the care of persons unfit to take charge of him. It is a great source of anxiety to me lest he should be suffering privation and bad treatment at this moment, when I, his grandfather, have abundance of worldly means, and have it in my power to rear him handsomely. I cannot help feeling that it is a fitting punishment for the cruel harshness with which I treated his mother. Now I am amassing wealth but I have no one to leave it to. I feel that I have small object in living. Yet I cannot give up the thought that my grandson is still living. I cannot help indulging the hope that some day, by the kind favor of Providence, he may be given back to me.

"If it will not be too much trouble to you and Mr. Fosdick, I shall feel indebted if you will still continue on the watch for the lost boy. Any expenses which you may incur, as I have already assured you, will be most cheerfully paid by your obliged friend and servant,

"HIRAM BATES."

While Richard was reading this letter, Mark listened attentively. Looking up, Richard observed this

"Did you ever meet with a boy named John Talbot, Mark?" he inquired.

"No," said Mark, "not *John* Talbot."

"Did you ever meet any boy named Talbot? It is not certain that the name is John."

"Talbot used to be my name," said Mark.

"Used to be your name!" exclaimed Richard, in surprise. "I thought it was Manton."

"Some of the boys gave me that name, because there was a story came out in one of the story papers about Mark Manton. After a while I got to calling myself so, but my real name is Mark Talbot."

"It would be strange if he should turn out to be the right boy after all, Dick," said Fosdick. "Where is the photograph? That will soon settle the question."

Richard Hunter opened his desk, and took out the card photograph which Mr. Bates had left with him.

"Mark," he said, "did you ever see any one who looked like that picture?"

Mark took the picture in his hand. No sooner did his eyes rest upon it than they filled with tears.

"That is my mother," he said. "Where did you get it?"

"Your mother! Are you sure?"

"Yes; I should know it anywhere, though it looks younger than she did."

"Do you know what her name was, before she was married?"

"Yes; she has told me often. It was Irene Bates."

"How strange!" exclaimed Richard and Fosdick together. "Mark," continued Richard, "I think you are the very boy I had been in search of for several months. I had succeeded without knowing it."

"Please tell me all about it," said Mark. "I don't understand."

"I have a great piece of good luck to announce to you, Mark. Your grandfather is a rich man, formerly in business in New York, but now a successful merchant in Milwaukie. He has no child, no descendant except yourself. He has been anxiously seeking for you, intending to give you all the advantages which his wealth can procure."

"Do you think I shall like him?" asked Mark, timidly.

"Yes; I think he will be very kind to you."

"But he was not kind to my mother. Although he was rich, he let her suffer."

"He has repented of this, and will try to make up to you his neglect to your mother."

Mark was still thoughtful. "If it had come sooner, my poor mother might still have been alive," he said.

"I think I had better telegraph to Mr. Bates to-morrow," said Richard. "The news will be so welcome that I don't like to keep it back a single day"

"Perhaps it will be better," said Fosdick. "You will have to give up your ward, Dick."

"Yes; but as it will be for his good, I will not object."

The next morning the following message was flashed over the wires to Milwaukie: —

"HIRAM BATES.

"Your grandson is found. He is well, and in my charge

"RICHARD HUNTER."

In the course of the forenoon, the following answer was received: —

"RICHARD HUNTER.

"How can I thank you! I take the next train for New York.

"HIRAM BATES."

On the afternoon succeeding, Mr. Bates entered Richard's counting-room. He clasped his hand with fervor.

"Mr. Hunter," he said, "I do not know how to thank you. Where is my boy?"

"I am just going up to the house," said Richard. "If you will accompany me, you shall soon see him."

"I am impatient to hear all the particulars," said Mr. Bates "Remember, I know nothing as yet. I only received your telegram announcing his discovery. When did you find him?"

"That is the strangest part of it," said Richard. "I found him sick just outside the office door several weeks since. I took him home, and when he recovered let him get a place in a bookstore; but, having become interested in him, I was unwilling to lose sight of him, and still kept him with me. All this while I was searching for your grandson, and had not the least idea that he was already found."

"How did you discover this at last?"

"By his recognition of his mother's photograph It was lucky you thought of leaving it with me."

"Is his name John?"

"He says his name is Mark, but for his last name he had adopted a different one, or I should have made the discovery sooner."

"How did he make a living before you found him? Poor boy!" said Mr. Bates, sighing, "I fear he must have suffered many privations."

"He was selling matches for some time, — what we call a match boy. He had suffered hardships. but I leave him to tell you his story himself."

"How does he feel about meeting me?" asked Mr. Bates.

"You are a stranger to him, and he naturally feels a little timid, but he will soon be reassured when he gets acquainted with you."

Mark had already arrived. As they entered the room, Mr. Bates said with emotion, "Is that he?"

"Yes, sir."

"Come here, Mark," he said, in a tone which took away Mark's apprehension. "Do you know who I am?"

"Are you my grandfather?"

"Yes, I have come to take care of you, and to see that you suffer no more from poverty."

Mr. Bates stooped down and pressed a kiss upon the boy's forehead.

"I can see Irene's look in his eyes," he said. "It is all the proof I need that he is my grand child."

It was arranged that in three days, for he had some business to transact, he should go back to Milwaukie. carrying Mark with him. He went round to Mr Baker's store the next morning with his grandson and explained to him why he should be obliged to withdraw him from his employ.

"I am sorry to lose him," said Mr. Baker. "He is quick and attentive to his duties, and has given me excellent satisfaction; but I am glad of his good fortune."

"It gives me pleasure to hear so good an account of him," said Mr. Bates. "Though he will be under no necessity of taking another situation, but will for several years devote himself to study, the same good qualities for which you give him credit will insure his satisfactory progress in school."

CHAPTER XXVI.

CONCLUSION.

It was not long before Mark felt quite at home with his grandfather. He no longer felt afraid of him, but began to look forward with pleasant anticipations to his journey West, and the life that was to open before him in Milwaukie. It was a relief to think that he would not now be obliged to take care of himself, but would have some one both able and willing to supply his wants, and provide him with a comfortable home.

He felt glad again that he was going to school. He remembered how anxious his poor mother had been that he should receive a good education, and now his grandfather had promised to send him to the best school in Milwaukie.

The next morning after their meeting, Mr. Bates took Mark to a large clothing establishment, and had him fitted out with new clothes in the most a liberal manner. He even bought him a silver watch, of which Mark felt very proud.

"Now, Mark," said his grandfather, "if there is any one that was kind to you when you were a poor match boy, I should like to do something to show my gratitude for their kindness. Can you think of any one?"

"Yes," said Mark; "there's Ben Gibson."

"And who is Ben Gibson?"

"He blacks boots down on Nassau Street. When I ran away from Mother Watson, who treated me so badly, he stood by me, and prevented her from getting hold of me again."

"Is there any one besides?"

"Yes," said Mark, after a pause; "there is Mrs. Flanagan. She lives in the same tenement-house where I used to. When I was almost starved she used to give me something to eat, though she was poor herself."

"I think we will call and see her first," said Mr Bates. "I am going to let you give her a hundred dollars."

"She will be delighted," said Mark, his eyes

sparkling with joy. "It will seem a fortune to her. Let us go at once"

Very well," said his grandfather. "Afterwards we will try to find your friend Ben."

I forgot to mention that Mr. Bates was stopping at the Fifth Avenue Hotel.

They took the University Place cars, which landed them at the junction of Barclay Street and Broadway. From thence it was but a short distance to Vandewater Street, where Mark lived when first introduced to the reader.

They climbed the broken staircase, and paused in front of Mrs. Flanagan's door.

Mark knocked.

Mrs. Flanagan opened the door, and stared with some surprise at her visitors.

"Don't you know me, Mrs. Flanagan?" asked Mark.

"Why, surely it isn't Mark, the little match boy?" said Mrs. Flanagan, amazed.

"Yes, it is. So you didn't know me?"

"And it's rale delighted I am to see you lookin' so fine. And who is this gentleman?"

"It is my grandfather, Mrs. Flanagan. I'm going out West to live with him."

Mrs. Flanagan dropped a courtesy to Mr. Bates who said, "My good woman, Mark tells me that you were kind to him when he stood in need of kindness"

"And did he say that?" said Mrs. Flanagan, her face beaming with pleasure. "Shure it was little I did for him, bein' poor myself; but that little he was heartily welcome to, and I'm delighted to think he's turned out so lucky. The ould woman trated him very bad. I used to feel as if I'd like to break her ould bones for her."

"Mark and I both want to thank you for your kindness to him, and he has a small gift to give you."

"Here it is," said Mark, drawing from his pocket a neat pocket-book, containing a roll of bills. "You'll find a hundred dollars inside, Mrs. Flanagan," he said. "I hope they will help you."

"A hundred dollars!" ejaculated Mrs. Flanagan, hardly believing her ears. "Does this good gentleman give me a hundred dollars!"

"No it is Mark's gift to you," said Mr. Bates.

"It's rich I am with so much money," said the

good woman. "May the saints bless you both! Now I can buy some clothes for the childer, and have plenty left beside. This is a happy day entirely. But won't you step in, and rest yourselves a bit? It's a poor room, but — "

"Thank you, Mrs. Flanagan," said Mr. Bates, "but we are in haste this morning. Whenever Mark comes to New York he shall come and see you."

They went downstairs, leaving Mrs. Flanagan so excited with her good fortune, that she left her work, and made a series of calls upon her neighbors, in which she detailed Mark's good fortune and her own.

"Now we'll go and find your friend, Ben Gibson," said Mr. Bates.

"I think we'll find him on Nassau Street," said Mark.

He was right.

In walking down Nassau Street on the east side, Mr. Bates was accosted by Ben himself.

"Shine yer boots?"

"How are you, Ben?" said Mark.

Ben stared in surprise till he recognized his old companion.

"Blest if it aint Mark," he said. "How you're gettin on!"

"Ben, this is my grandfather," said Mark.

"Well, you're a lucky chap," said Ben, enviously "I wish I could find a rich grandfather. I don't believe I ever had a grandfather."

"How are you getting on, my lad?" inquired Mr. Bates.

"Middlin'," said Ben. "I haven't laid by a fortun' yet."

"No, I suppose not. How do you like blacking boots?"

"Well, there's other things I might like better," said Ben, — "such as bein' a rich merchant; but that takes rather more capital than blackin' boots."

"I see you are an original," said Mr. Bates smiling.

"Am I?" said Ben. "Well, I'm glad of it, though I didn't know it before. I hope it aint anything very bad."

"Mark says you treated him kindly when he lived about the street."

"It wasn't much," said Ben.

"I want to do something for you. What shall I do?"

"Well," said Ben, "I should like a new brush. This is most worn out."

"How would you like to go to Milwaukie with Mark, if I will get you a place there?"

"Do you mean it?" said Ben, incredulously.

"Certainly."

"I haven't any money to pay for goin' out there."

"I will take care of that," said Mr. Bates.

"Then I'll go," said Ben, "and I'm much obliged to you. Mark, you're a brick, and so's your grandfather. I never expected to have such good luck."

"Then you must begin to make arrangements at once. Mark, here is some money. You may go with Ben, see that he takes a good bath, and then buy him some clothes. I am obliged to leave you to do it, as I must attend to some business in Wall Street. I shall expect to see you both at the Fifth Avenue Hotel at two o'clock."

At two o'clock, Mr. Bates found the two boys awaiting him. There was a great change in Ben's appearance. He had faithfully submitted to the bath, and bloomed out in a tasteful suit of clothes, selected by Mark. Mark had taken him besides to a barber's and had his long hair cut. So he now made quite a presentable appearance, though he felt very awkward in his new clothes.

"It don't seem natural to be clean," he confessed to Mark.

"You'll get used to it after a while," said Mark, laughing.

"Maybe I will; but I miss my old clothes. They seemed more comfortable."

The next day they were to start. Ben remained at the hotel with his friend Mark, feeling, it must be confessed, a curious sensation at his unusual position.

They went to make a farewell call on Richard Hunter.

"Mr. Hunter," said Mr. Bates, "money will not pay you for the service you have done me, but I shall be glad if you will accept this cheque."

Richard saw that it was a cheque for a thousand dollars.

"Thank you for your liberality, Mr. Bates," he said; "but I do not deserve it."

"Let me be the judge of that."

"I will accept it on one condition."

"Name it, Mr. Hunter."

"That you will allow me to give it to the Newsboys' Lodge, where I once found shelter, and where so many poor boys are now provided for."

"I will give an equal sum to that institution," said Mr. Bates, "and I thank you for reminding me of it. As for this money, oblige me by keeping it yourself."

"Then," said Richard, "I will keep it as a charity fund, and whenever I have an opportunity of helping along a boy who is struggling upward as I once had to struggle, I will do it."

"A noble resolution, Mr. Hunter! You have found out the best use of money."

Mark is now at an excellent school in Milwaukie, pursuing his studies. He is the joy and solace of his grandfather's life, hitherto sad and lonely, and is winning the commendation of his teachers by his devotion to study. A place was found for Ben Gibson, where he had some advantages of education, and he is likely to do well. He has been persuaded by

Mark to leave off smoking, — a habit which he had formed in the streets of New York. The shrewdness which his early experiences taught him will be likely to benefit him in the business career which lies before him.

Every year Mark sends a substantial present to Mrs Flanagan, under his grandfather's direction, and thus makes the worthy woman's life much more comfortable and easy. From time to time Mark receives a letter from Richard Hunter, who has not lost his interest in the little match boy who was once his ward.

So the trials of Mark, the Match Boy, as far as they proceeded from poverty and privation, are at an end. He has found a comfortable and even luxurious home, and a relative whose great object in life is to study his happiness. I hope that the record of his struggles will be read with interest by my young readers, and shall hope to meet them all again in the next volume of this series, which will be called:

ROUGH AND READY;

OR,

LIFE AMONG THE NEW YORK NEWSBOYS.

A writer for boys should have an abundant sympathy with them. He should be able to enter into their plans, hopes, and aspirations. He should learn to look upon life as they do. Boys object to be written down to. A boy's heart opens to the man or writer who understands him.

—From *Writing Stories for Boys*, by Horatio Alger, Jr.

LUCK AND PLUCK SERIES—Second Series.

4 vols. $4.00

Try and Trust.
Bound to Rise.
Risen from the Ranks.
Herbert Carter's Legacy.

BRAVE AND BOLD SERIES.

4 vols. BY HORATIO ALGER, JR. $4.00

Brave and Bold.
Jack's Ward.
Shifting for Himself.
Wait and Hope.

NEW WORLD SERIES.

3 vols. BY HORATIO ALGER, JR. $3.00

Digging for Gold. Facing the World. In a New World.

VICTORY SERIES.

3 vols. BY HORATIO ALGER, JR. $3.00

Only an Irish Boy. Adrift in the City.
Victor Vane, or the Young Secretary.

FRANK AND FEARLESS SERIES.

3 vols. BY HORATIO ALGER, JR. $3.00

Frank Hunter's Peril. Frank and Fearless.
The Young Salesman.

GOOD FORTUNE LIBRARY.

3 vols. BY HORATIO ALGER, JR. $3.00

Walter Sherwood's Probation. A Boy's Fortune.
The Young Bank Messenger.

RUPERT'S AMBITION.

1 vol. BY HORATIO ALGER, JR. $1.00

JED, THE POOR-HOUSE BOY.

1 vol. BY HORATIO ALGER, JR. $1.00

HARRY CASTLEMON.

HOW I CAME TO WRITE MY FIRST BOOK.

WHEN I was sixteen years old I belonged to a composition class. It was our custom to go on the recitation seat every day with clean slates, and we were allowed ten minutes to write seventy words on any subject the teacher thought suited to our capacity. One day he gave out "What a Man Would See if He Went to Greenland." My heart was in the matter, and before the ten minutes were up I had one side of my slate filled. The teacher listened to the reading of our compositions, and when they were all over he simply said: "Some of you will make your living by writing one of these days." That gave me something to ponder upon. I did not say so out loud, but I knew that my composition was as good as the best of them. By the way, there was another thing that came in my way just then. I was reading at that time one of Mayne Reid's works which I had drawn from the library, and I pondered upon it as much as I did upon what the teacher said to me. In introducing Swartboy to his readers he made use of this expression: "No visible change was observable in Swartboy's countenance." Now, it occurred to me that if a man of his education could make such a blunder as that and still write a book, I ought to be able to do it, too. I went home that very day and began a story, "The Old Guide's Narrative," which was sent to the *New York Weekly*, and came back, respectfully declined. It was written on both sides of the sheets but I didn't know that this was against the rules. Nothing abashed, I began another, and receiving some instruction, from a friend of mine who was a clerk in a book store, I wrote it on only one side of the paper. But mind you, he didn't know what I was doing. Nobody knew it; but one day, after a hard Saturday's work—the other boys had been out skating on the brick-pond—I shyly broached the subject to my mother. I felt the need of some sympathy. She listened in amazement, and then said: "Why, do you think you could write a book like that?" That settled the matter, and from that day no one knew what I was up to until I sent the first four volumes of Gunboat Series to my father. Was it work? Well, yes; it was hard work, but each week I had the satisfaction of seeing the manuscript grow until the "Young Naturalist" was all complete.

—Harry Castlemon in the Writer.

ROUGHING IT SERIES.

*3 vols. BY HARRY CASTLEMON. $3.00

George in Camp. George at the Fort.
George at the Wheel.

ROD AND GUN SERIES.

3 vols. BY HARRY CASTLEMON. $3.00

Don Gordon's Shooting Box. The Young Wild Fowlers.
Rod and Gun Club.

GO-AHEAD SERIES.

3 vols. BY HARRY CASTLEMON. $3.00

Tom Newcombe. Go-Ahead. No Moss.

WAR SERIES.

6 vols. BY HARRY CASTLEMON. $6.00

True to His Colors. Marcy the Blockade-Runner.
Rodney the Partisan. Marcy the Refugee.
Rodney the Overseer. Sailor Jack the Trader.

HOUSEBOAT SERIES.

3 vols. BY HARRY CASTLEMON. $3.00

The Houseboat Boys. The Mystery of Lost River Cañon.
The Young Game Warden.

AFLOAT AND ASHORE SERIES.

3 vols. BY HARRY CASTLEMON. $3.00

Rebellion in Dixie. A Sailor in Spite of Himself.
The Ten-Ton Cutter.

THE PONY EXPRESS SERIES.

3 vol. BY HARRY CASTLEMON. $3.00

The Pony Express Rider. The White Beaver.
Carl, The Trailer.

EDWARD S. ELLIS.

EDWARD S. ELLIS, the popular writer of boys' books, is a native of Ohio, where he was born somewhat more than a half-century ago. His father was a famous hunter and rifle shot, and it was doubtless his exploits and those of his associates, with their tales of adventure which gave the son his taste for the breezy backwoods and for depicting the stirring life of the early settlers on the frontier.

Mr. Ellis began writing at an early age and his work was acceptable from the first. His parents removed to New Jersey while he was a boy and he was graduated from the State Normal School and became a member of the faculty while still in his teens. He was afterward principal of the Trenton High School, a trustee and then superintendent of schools. By that time his services as a writer had become so pronounced that he gave his entire attention to literature. He was an exceptionally successful teacher and wrote a number of text-books for schools, all of which met with high favor. For these and his historical productions, Princeton College conferred upon him the degree of Master of Arts.

The high moral character, the clean, manly tendencies and the admirable literary style of Mr. Ellis' stories have made him as popular on the other side of the Atlantic as in this country. A leading paper remarked some time since, that no mother need hesitate to place in the hands of her boy any book written by Mr. Ellis. They are found in the leading Sunday-school libraries, where, as may well be believed, they are in wide demand and do much good by their sound, wholesome lessons which render them as acceptable to parents as to their children. All of his books published by Henry T. Coates & Co. are re-issued in London, and many have been translated into other languages. Mr. Ellis is a writer of varied accomplishments, and, in addition to his stories, is the author of historical works, of a number of pieces of popular music and has made several valuable inventions. Mr. Ellis is in the prime of his mental and physical powers, and great as have been the merits of his past achievements, there is reason to look for more brilliant productions from his pen in the near future.

DEERFOOT SERIES.

3 vols. BY EDWARD S. ELLIS. $3.00

Hunters of the Ozark. The Last War Trail.
Camp in the Mountains.

LOG CABIN SERIES.

3 vols. BY EDWARD S. ELLIS. $3.00

Lost Trail. Footprints in the Forest.
Camp-Fire and Wigwam.

BOY PIONEER SERIES.

3 vols. BY EDWARD S. ELLIS. $3.00

Ned in the Block-House. Ned on the River.
Ned in the Woods.

THE NORTHWEST SERIES.

3 vols. BY EDWARD S. ELLIS. $3.00

Two Boys in Wyoming. Cowmen and Rustlers.
A Strange Craft and its Wonderful Voyage.

BOONE AND KENTON SERIES.

3 vols. BY EDWARD S. ELLIS. $3.00

Shod with Silence. In the Days of the Pioneers.
Phantom of the River.

IRON HEART, WAR CHIEF OF THE IROQUOIS.

1 vol. BY EDWARD S. ELLIS. $1.00

THE NEW DEERFOOT SERIES.

3 vols. BY EDWARD S. ELLIS. $3.00

Deerfoot in the Forest. Deerfoot on the Prairie.
Deerfoot in the Mountains.

J. T. TROWBRIDGE.

NEITHER as a writer does he stand apart from the great currents of life and select some exceptional phase or odd combination of circumstances. He stands on the common level and appeals to the universal heart, and all that he suggests or achieves is on the plane and in the line of march of the great body of humanity.

The Jack Hazard series of stories, published in the late *Our Young Folks*, and continued in the first volume of *St. Nicholas*, under the title of "Fast Friends," is no doubt destined to hold a high place in this class of literature. The delight of the boys in them (and of their seniors, too) is well founded. They go to the right spot every time. Trowbridge knows the heart of a boy like a book, and the heart of a man, too, and he has laid them both open in these books in a most successful manner. Apart from the qualities that render the series so attractive to all young readers, they have great value on account of their portraitures of American country life and character. The drawing is wonderfully accurate, and as spirited as it is true. The constable, Sellick, is an original character, and as minor figures where will we find anything better than Miss Wansey, and Mr. P. Pipkin, Esq. The picture of Mr. Dink's school, too, is capital, and where else in fiction is there a better nick-name than that the boys gave to poor little Stephen Treadwell, "Step Hen," as he himself pronounced his name in an unfortunate moment when he saw it in print for the first time in his lesson in school.

On the whole, these books are very satisfactory, and afford the critical reader the rare pleasure of the works that are just adequate, that easily fulfill themselves and accomplish all they set out to do.—*Scribner's Monthly.*

CPSIA information can be obtained
at www.ICGtesting.com
Printed in the USA
LVOW13s1024020617
536727LV00018B/322/P